Just the Facts

Just the Facts

A novel

Ellen Sherman

SHE WRITES PRESS

Published 2015
Printed in the United States of America
ISBN: 978-1-63152-993-1
Library of Congress Control Number: 2015933755

For information, address:
She Writes Press
1563 Solano Ave #546
Berkeley, CA 94707

She Writes Press is a division of SparkPoint Studio, LLC.

Some blurbs at the beginning of chapters are excerpted from, or inspired by, items that appeared in the "Police Beat" sections of *The Maryland Gazette* and/ or *The Evening Capital* in 1978 or 1979.

In honor of my mother, Carol Sherman
and for Chris, forever

What a curiosity it was to hold a pen—nothing but a small pointed stick, after all, oozing its hieroglyphic puddles... An immersion into the living language: all at once this cleanliness, this capacity, this power to make a history, to tell, to explain. To retrieve, to reprieve!
To lie.

Cynthia Ozick, *The Shawl*

Chapter One
Fall Forward

Bandits Rob Bar

Two masked bandits, armed with a shotgun and a rifle, allegedly held up a Crownsville tavern Sunday night, locked the patrons and employees in the men's room, and made off with $63.27 from the cash register, county police said.

South Falls, Md., Sept. 1978—I considered myself more fortunate than others. But when the kitchen phone rang at six a.m., I sensed everything was about to change. My stomach tightened as I ran downstairs and grabbed it, knowing it could only be for me.

"Slanecrash—need night way," was what I heard.

"Little Bill? What?"

"A small plane crashed at BWI! You need to get there right away! A photographer will meet you!"

It was definitely my assistant editor, using way too many exclamation points. I nodded, shivering in my underwear and T-shirt. I'd been fast asleep. My two housemates would still be sleeping; they slept like lumberjacks. Were lumberjacks heavy sleepers?

"Nora? Still there?"

"Yeah, sorry. Say it one more time?"

Now he spoke in ridiculous fashion, pausing after each word.

"Okay. I'm off," I said, rubbing my eyes. No doubt Little Bill had picked me for this assignment because I lived the closest to Baltimore-Washington International Airport, and had driven there to interview the newly crowned Miss America the week before, on my second day at the paper. She had been en route to the Dominican Republic to help out at a school for severely handicapped children, and had been delightful to interview, so enthusiastic it seemed like she was still competing. But this. Talk about throwing me right in there.

A press officer greeted the reporters as we arrived, corralling us into a small room as cold as a meat locker. "You will not be permitted to view the wreckage," he said, and inwardly I said, "Amen," even though I knew this was the wrong response.

I jotted down his answers while the others asked questions.

It is not immediately clear what caused the crash, which occurred shortly after five a.m. The family is not available for comment.

Thank G-d, I mumbled.

There was an eyewitness: *A man driving to the airport saw the plane spiraling down. He ran into the adjacent woods to try to help and saw the remains of the pilot slumped inside the cockpit.* The press officer looked up, scanned the faces of the reporters and cameramen. *The plane was badly damaged,* he added, daring us to imagine what condition the pilot's body was in. Goose bumps broke out on my arms—again.

A fire at the crash scene was extinguished.

Even though the aircraft was a two-seater, for us this was a big-gish story, so a freelance photographer named Stu had been sent to join me. He was able to go as far as the cordoned area at the base of the woods, reporting back that he had shot some photos of the "crumpled" plane, although probably from too great a distance. He gave me the roll of film, saying, "Take that directly to *The Courier*. You'll write the story there."

The Annapolis Evening Courier was our sister paper, the daily. I worked at the semi-weekly, but important stories appeared in both. This would be my first in the big paper, a fact that intensified my nerves.

To me, Stu seemed blank and dispassionate, but then I noticed the tension in his eyes. "The air is still wriggly—you know, the way it gets above a barbeque. And it smelled really funky out there, something I can't describe," he said. "Don't take too long to finish up here," he added as he left.

I hoped I was finished now. I walked out of the press room feeling several things at once: relief that all I'd had to do was listen, that I didn't have to ask any hard questions or see the wreckage; but also ashamed—I was still such a baby.

My father used to yell at me when I ran out of the room during the violent parts of movies. "It's only a movie," he would say, but for me everything was real. What got me most was not so much the blood and gore, but rather the pain and horror on people's faces, the intolerable suffering.

So here, at the perimeter of disaster, I was grateful to be limited to a perfunctory job. I ran toward my car, but just before reaching it, stopped, out of breath, something compelling me to turn and survey the empty runway which gave away nothing about what had transpired so close by. A maintenance man wearing a fluorescent orange vest stood beside a row of small planes. I headed over to ask if he had seen anything.

Jeff Grissom, mechanic and airport employee, said he was standing on Runway 7 a few minutes after five when he 'saw that poor little plane plummet after its second attempt to land.' He removed his cap, held it to his chest. 'It was absolutely awful,' he said. 'Took my breath away.'

Cool-ish morning, end of September. The fog, ever-present in the early mornings and after sunset in this county that bordered the Chesapeake, finally dissipated as I made my way to *The Courier*'s offices. Another beautiful day, belying a million tragedies.

The Courier was a majestic facility compared to *The Anne Arundel Record*, my paper. The newsroom was bustling. Roger, the managing editor, told me to use the desk of someone named McCord, gently seating me in McCord's swivel chair. Roger was younger and hipper than my editor, Big Bill. I had met him on my job-search trip. In fact, it was Roger who had directed me to *The Record*, suggesting I get my feet wet there before attempting to work at a daily.

I started to type and the story poured out.

A small, single-engine Cessna plane spiraled out of the foggy sky and crashed in the heavily wooded area not far from Runway 7 at Baltimore-Washington International Airport (BWI) early this morning, according to James Larson, airport spokesman.

The pilot, John Baldwin, 31, of Arnold, MD, was pronounced dead at the scene, as was his passenger, Mindy Baldwin, 29, the pilot's sister. Ms. Baldwin also resided in Arnold.

Eyewitness's account, Jeff Grissom's account...

As I finished writing, I was flooded with sadness and disturbing thoughts. A brother and sister, two years apart, same as my brother and me. My mother used to call us, Jake and me, the Bickersons. "You can't stand to be together, but you can't stand to be apart," she liked to say.

I missed Jake a lot, and I also was reminded of how much our dad loved planes. He had once told me that, if he could do his life over again, he would become a pilot. He had been so disappointed not to serve in the military in "War Two" (as he called it)—exempt for various reasons, not the least of which was that he needed to support his mother and three younger sisters.

"All done?" A handsome guy with unruly black hair startled me out of my reverie. He was standing, arms folded, leaning against the top of McCord's cubicle.

"Mr. McCord, I presume?"

He shook his head no.

"I'm not quite done. I want to check it one more time. This is my debut in the daily." I knew the story would run on the front page, top of the fold.

"Connor Hannah," the guy said, extending his hand. "I've been reading your stuff. Not bad for a rookie. How's Old Bill treating you?"

"Fine. He's pretty nice."

"You think so?"

I smiled. Almost all of *The Courier* reporters began at *The Record*. It was like a minor-league feeder team. Connor Hannah looked to be in his mid-thirties, making him one of the oldest on the reportorial staff. I read *The Courier* religiously, especially his stuff, and he was hands-down the best in my opinion, an excellent news reporter who also wrote humorous features.

I loved his lyrical name, so symmetrical with all those "o's," "n's," "a's," and "h's." He wrote with a lilt, too, like he grew up gallivanting in a glen. *The Courier* had just finished running a series describing his participation in a class filled with hilarious, if somewhat improbable, characters learning to line jump from a plane. On the day of the big event, he had broken his wrist upon landing.

No matter, I am on the ground, and almost in one piece. My fellow jumpers take a long time getting up, but at a glance, they also seem mostly whole. We stand together, as grateful to be alive as patients coming out of anesthesia—Carlos holding his head, Kathleen her hip, and I my wrist, which certainly is no longer properly aligned. Then Captain Kyle asks, and we all nod our heads "Sure." We'd like to do it again.

I had been wondering what he looked like. He had a swarthy complexion and a constellation of dark beauty marks on his face, which I found very appealing, particularly this one dot at the lower corner of his left eye.

"Hey, how's your wrist?" I asked. "That was a great series."

"Not too bad now. I broke my radius bone. It's almost healed." He unbuttoned his shirt cuff to reveal a wrist and forearm wrapped in gauze.

"Whoa—that's a lot of tape!"

"It only hurts when I type," he said. Another guy with a winning smile.

When I finished, Roger told me to wait while he read over my article, right in front of me. "Great. Thanks for your help," he said.

I strutted over to Connor's desk to say goodbye. He didn't hear me approach, intent on making sense out of chaos, these little slips of paper with scribbles on them, which were everywhere. I tapped his shoulder and he swung around.

We stared at each other for a bit.

"Oh, so long, Plowright," he said with a wink. "Keep knocking 'em dead with the obits!"

Oy, I thought, but I lingered a few seconds longer, hoping he'd ask for my number. Well, at least he knew where to find me.

In the middle of the month, I had moved to Maryland with one suitcase, an electric typewriter, and a large cardboard box filled with typing paper, legal pads, Wite-Out, and a bundle of pens I had taken from my dad's store. Down the side, they read: "Plow*right*. Plow *far*."

My father had been inspired by the words of Thomas Carlyle: "Go as far as you can see; when you get there you'll be able to see farther." He was the most practical person I'd ever known, my father, having lived a life bound by commitments and responsibilities. Yet on my behalf he was a dreamer, urging me to "reach for the stars." He'd had my mom embroider that on a throw pillow for me when I left for college, thankfully without the transistor-radio logo for Plowright Electronics.

It was a tall order.

When he had started his business, before I was born, my father changed his name from Plutz to Plowright, a good move. I thought my name, Nora, suggested someone who strove for change, like Nora in *A Doll's House*; or perhaps someone acerbically assertive, *a la* Nora Charles in *The Thin Man*. At the least, Nora Anne Plowright sounded credible, someone who wanted to try hard, be a good person, do the right thing. Someone who could look you in the eye. Someone destined to make something out of her life?

At the last minute, my mom persuaded me to take the pillows, blanket, linens, desk blotter, and a few lamps from my childhood bedroom. This was disconcerting; hopefully, I could still come home to visit. My dad presented me with the keys to a used 1971 Chevrolet Caprice, my college graduation present. We were in the middle of a gas crisis and this bruiser of a used car was humming when it got ten miles per gallon, but obviously fuel efficiency was not my dad's chief concern. He wanted me to be safe, and felt I was better off traveling by boat.

Initially, I stayed at a Holiday Inn about ten minutes from the newspaper's offices, and on my first day of work I loitered at a Dunkin' Donuts, reading *The New York Times* and *The Record*, drinking my first cup of coffee ever ("black" for this hard-bitten reporter) and demolishing two vanilla kreme donuts (the "k" guaranteeing they were 100 percent ersatz). I skimmed through the papers with this refrain in my head: "What have I done? What have I done? I don't know how to be a reporter. I'm afraid"—to the tune of a camp color-war song. Then I looked at my watch. I was about to be late.

The *Record's* staff was small. There was the editor-in-chief, Mr. Gilhooley, who went by Big Bill; the assistant editor, Little Bill, about five-four, early thirties, who was also a prolific general assignment reporter; and the people in their twenties: Catherine, news reporter; Tim, sports reporter; and now me, an insecure news reporter because when it came down to it, I wasn't sure I could jump into the fray. I was afraid it would be like when I played field hockey in high school: I was fast and always near the ball, but couldn't quite bring myself to jab my stick in there, to really mix it up, and possibly get badly bruised.

"What makes you qualified to be a newspaper reporter?" Big Bill had asked when he interviewed me.

"I think I have a nose for news," I said, inching forward in my chair like I was telling him a secret, hoping to appear earnest. You *could* make these things up. "Also, I'm really good with people, which is conducive to getting them to talk to me, open up to me."

Me, me, me....

Bill Gilhooley, venerable editor-in-chief of *The Anne Arundel Record* (America's oldest newspaper, as it happened), raised his salty gray, bushy eyebrows and couldn't have looked more skeptical. My relevant experience was paltry; I had written for my high school sports page and a few articles for my college paper. He glanced at the clips I'd provided: "Bulldogs Outlast Warriors," "School Prez Encourages Interface with Community."

"Why do you want to work at a paper?" he asked, his eyes now riveted on a mound of chewing gum clotted with debris on the sole of his worn Top-Sider.

"Well, I've always loved to write, and I think I'm pretty good at it. One day I'd like to be a novelist, but I'm twenty-two—I need some experience. Hell, I need a lot of experience, and I also need to support myself, not to mention get out of my parents' house."

Shouldn't have said "hell," obviously. I smiled sweetly.

He examined my resume again. "My son just moved to New Jersey. Verona. That's near your hometown, right?"

"Right next door!"

"Love those Tudor houses," Big Bill said, all sunshine and light now.

Little Bill was from "the deep South," while Catherine hailed from Iowa. Big Bill and Tim actually grew up in Severna Park, where the paper was based. All any of them had ever wanted was to work on a newspaper.

After the intros that first day, Big Bill had called me into his small office—the rest of us shared one large newsroom. He had typed out directions to the police department and said I was to get there at eight on the dot every morning to go through the reports and select items for the police blotter. I was thinking that his thick, graying hair and a few days' worth of stubble made him look like a ship's captain.

"The funeral homes send us releases and you need to write these up every day, too," Big Bill said. "These are two good places to start." He handed me a stack of back issues by way of example, and three funeral-home notices to work on right away. I was astonished that he wanted me to just dive in like that, that I wouldn't be trailing one of the reporters for a week or so. Welcome to the Show.

"Also, I'll give you some leads at the beginning, but as you get acquainted with the different towns in our catchment area, we'll expect you to start generating stories on your own," my editor continued.

"Catchment" was a new one to me, and I wasn't crazy about that other word: expect.

Now, my ninth day on the job, I had covered headline news. And the day had barely begun. Eight thirty! I needed to do the police blotter.

With its large reception desk in the entrance hall, long lines of lockers, and antiseptic blue-green paint, the Police Department reminded me of my junior high school. The other day, when entering the front hall, I had seen policemen escorting men in chains—chains on their ankles and hands cuffed at their waists, like in the movies.

Usually I was the only reporter in the press room, and Sergeant Jack Johnson, the press officer, and I had taken to each other instantly.

"They sent me to that plane crash," I said.

"You?"

I shrugged. "It was intense, but I handled it."

"Happens sometimes."

Jack seemed to appreciate my enthusiasm, although he couldn't get over how little I knew. After reading my very first police report, I asked "What's D.O.A.?" and he literally fell off his chair laughing.

"Girl," he said, righting himself and brushing off what looked like sawdust. Pencil shavings? "Where'd you say you came from? I thought you were a city girl." I was filled with regret that I had never watched cop shows on TV, but I let him slide on calling me "girl" since I was going to need his help.

This morning, I studied a long list of contents stolen in a "grand" larceny (more than one thousand dollars worth of goods) of a residence: gold jewelry, a fur coat, three televisions. "What's a dildo?" I asked.

Jack howled. "Girlie, you're killing me. I thought you were a college grad?"

"Girlie" crossed the line, and I scowled at Jack. He had the worst sideburns—too thick and too long. Too red.

"Another hold-up at the Circle K," Jack said, showing me the report. Several of these convenience stores lined Route 3, a truck route that ran along the county corridor, and the favorite pastime seemed to be holding them up with sawed-off shotguns, whatever those were. I'd always enjoyed ducking into convenience stores, browsing through all the stuff: colored paper clips, Styrofoam cups, clothespins, safety pins, electrical adapters, candy made by companies I'd never heard of. Who used safety pins anyway? You got about one hundred in a pack when maybe you would need three in your entire life.

I was learning a lot reading the police reports. Initially, I was stunned that so many people had NMN in their name. John NMN Carter. Edward NMN Lee. "What's this NMN? Some kind of Korean clan?" I asked Jack, which set him shrieking with laughter again.

"*No Middle Name*, girl. N-M-N: No Middle Name. That's what it means."

Everyone arrested was "released on his own recognizance." I didn't ask Jack what the hell that meant—I could look that up later, too. There were so many masked criminals wandering around Maryland, worse than long-ago Australia.

Driving to my newsroom, my nerves caught up with me again. Initial theories were that the small Cessna had hit a cross wind, causing it to roll over. It most certainly had clipped trees coming down.

I was thankful my father had never gotten his wish and learned to fly. Though he had missed out on active duty in World War II, he had been a civilian volunteer, trained to spot planes in the event of an air strike. My Aunt Rita, his youngest sister, had told me recently that my dad loved to build model planes as a boy, wonderful models. Their dad, a grandfather I had never known because he died when my father was fifteen, was a tailor, and one day he asked my father to give him one of the models for a customer.

"It was this beautiful, giant military plane," Rita said. "Your father spent hours and hours on it, putting on the decals just so. He was meticulous with his models, and so fond of them." When my father pleaded to keep the plane, my grandfather had smashed it into the wall, saying, "Now no one will have it." Allegedly. Hard to believe his father could be that cruel. But though he was always nice to me, my father could be a little scary too.

Big Bill was always at his desk early, and he looked up and nodded when he saw me come in. From his small office he had a straight line of vision to my desk, and I wondered if he'd set things up like that intentionally, always having the new kid in his sights. "Heard you did a good job today," he called out.

"Thanks," I called back, heading over to the coffee station. I drank a whole cup standing there, then poured another to take back to my desk—it was there for the taking—where I began typing up my police blurbs with great focus. They were rather formulaic. I followed examples in our back issues.

Fiery Love Triangle

County police have filed assault charges against a 24-year-old Suffern Park man who allegedly fired a pistol at his roommate after an argument over a woman.

The obits were even more straightforward:

Jacqueline Hubbard, 73, of Ocean City, died Aug. 15 at Johns Hopkins Hospital after a lengthy illness. Miss Hubbard, who attended St. Jerome High School, was a cosmetologist and Girl Scout Leader in Stockville for many years. She enjoyed ceramics.

After a while Little Bill arrived. Since he worked late laying out our paper two nights a week, he took his time getting in.

"Thanks for covering this morning. How'd it go?" he asked, picking up a stack of papers.

"That was something," I said.

He gave me a sympathetic smile.

Soon Tim was there, too, and I admired how he got right down to work. It seemed he was always playing catch-up, needing to get everything written up fast so he could spend his afternoons and evenings attending the next set of games at local high schools and colleges.

But Catherine was the most impressive. She often had three lengthy pieces in each issue, all starting on the front page. Generally, she was out on assignments until three in the afternoon, then at her desk typing with gusto so she could leave at a reasonable hour. According to Tim, she was engaged to the county executive's press secretary, which sounded like a conflict of interest to me.

My large consumption of coffee made me antsy. I couldn't sit still. Also, I felt self-conscious conducting phone interviews with the others around, something that didn't seem to bother them at all. I spent a lot of time listening in on the phone conversations of my colleagues.

So far, I was sure everyone could tell I was serious, and I made an effort to look busy, typing journal entries about my new surroundings, or letters to my brother and friends, instead of writing up articles between nine and five. I managed to do some phone interviews during the day—I had to—and found it easy to dash off the police blurbs and obits, but it wasn't until after the others left that I settled down and composed anything of substance.

It was a thrill to see my police blurbs in print, and I read my published obits over and over. Tonight, the plane crash piece would appear in *The Evening Courier,* and if I could get them ready, I would have two more bylines in *The Record* tomorrow: one about the banning of potato chips from lunch platters at Devon Elementary School, the other about the theft of a well-trained cockatiel from The Bird House on Ritchie Highway.

We all used IBM Selectrics and we typed on white sheets with pink margins and *The Anne Arundel Record* logo at the bottom. A pink sheet beneath produced a carbon copy. At the top of my articles I wrote:

By Nora Plowright
Staff Writer

If we made mistakes, we literally X'd over the words: XXXX. And at the end of every piece, we typed "-30-."

Little Bill had just told Tim how he'd sent me to the crash scene that morning.

"Really? You're so lucky," Tim said. "A byline in the daily and you've been here, what, two weeks? And with virtually no experience going in. Jeez, no one does that."

Like I said, I was more fortunate than most.

Chapter Two
Anne Arundel County

Shooting at 7-Eleven

A man wearing a black ski mask and wielding a sawed-off shotgun allegedly fired three bullets into the chest of the proprietor of the Crofton 7-Eleven, leaving the man in critical condition, county police said.

One of the perks of being a reporter is that you can get the classifieds a few days in advance of their publication. That was how I found the house on Carroll Drive. "Two rooms to rent in warm and cozy four-bedroom house. Women only." South Falls was a working-class town squeezed between two truck routes. The downtown was so rinky-dink that its parking meters took pennies, but the house was part of a tidy, 1950s development on a tree-lined street.

"Tidy development" and "tree-lined street" were journalistic tics. I pledged to keep my observations fresh.

Seventy-Eight Carroll Drive had cobalt blue wall-to-wall carpeting throughout the first and second floors and a chrome and mock leather living-room set, but Linda and Robin, the two tenants, were friendly and warm, as advertised. There were three bedrooms upstairs, and I was offered the third for one hundred and twenty-five dollars per month, utilities included. It was about ten feet by twelve feet, but that was plenty of space for someone with no furniture.

Robin, eighteen, occupied the second room, and Linda, thirty-two, the master bedroom. The three bedrooms and small bathroom were painted other shades of blue.

"There's another, larger room in the basement," Linda said, "if you prefer. It's more private down there."

The basement was a bit dank and cloaked with chocolate-brown carpeting; it covered the floor and ran halfway up the walls. To me, it represented the dismal, ever-muddy earth while the blues on the first and second floors were the sky, the stratosphere, a transcendent universe where anything was possible.

"I'd much rather live up there," I said, pointing.

Right at the outset, Linda disclosed that she was an executive secretary and a divorcée (all the first-floor furniture was hers). Robin, a waitress, had dropped out of high school and left her parents' home on the Eastern Shore two years ago. The two women seemed to get along great and thought it was "cool" that I was a reporter and planned to stay awhile.

The bedroom in the basement had apparently been unoccupied for a long time until Jennifer arrived a week after me. Originally from Texas, she was a flight attendant, and her suitability seemed almost prophetic because, when I first saw her, she was wearing a brown skirt suit—Delta's colors—and her luggage was the same shade of chocolate as the carpeting in the cavernous basement.

I was the only one who was Jewish at the house, and possibly at the papers, too. Religion had not come up at either place, but for some reason I mentioned it to my housemates as we sat around one night.

"I thought you might be," Linda said, quickly adding, "We certainly don't care," to which the others nodded.

A few weeks later, I was alone in the house. Jennifer had flown to Tokyo and beyond, and Robin and Linda were in the Bahamas, on a hurricane-season package they had booked months ago. In the living room, a series of large windows, bench height to ceiling, made me feel vulnerable, and above the bathtub, an overgrown spider plant resembled a hairy monster, especially as it cast a long, fuzzy shadow on the wall when the nightlight was on, like tarantulas were crawling all over it.

I had always been afraid of staying by myself overnight, but had no options here. I came home before dark every night that week, and left lights on all night in the kitchen, living room, upstairs hall, and Linda's bedroom, reasoning that would-be invaders would believe the house was occupied by insomniacs. Police beat had already taught me that criminals were opportunists who didn't typically seek confrontation. Besides, if someone was coming for me, I wanted to see. I spent most of my time holed up in my room. It was the loneliest week of my life.

Late one afternoon, I was in the kitchen on the phone with my folks when I heard a thunderous crash, as if a china cabinet had toppled over—only Linda didn't own a china cabinet. Peering around the door into the dining room, I saw a huge leg with a scruffy work boot attached to it sticking through a window.

"Gotta go," I said, dropping the receiver on the table and dashing out the front door, across the street to a house where a family of four lived. I had waved to the mom over there a few times.

"Can I use your phone? I need to call the police," I said, my voice really high.

"The pol-lice!" the lady's toddler daughter said, orange macaroni and cheese all over her face.

"Someone's breaking into the house," I mouthed to the mom.

"Huh?" she said.

We waited, staring out her living-room windows, and in less than ten minutes, two police cars pulled up, sirens whirling. Four cops surrounded my house with their guns drawn, which seemed excessive even under the circumstances.

At that moment, a man walked out of the front door with his arms raised high in the air. He was grinning.

"You're kidding," I said. "That's my landlord, I think—I only met him once. Thanks, Debbie. I have to go." I ran into the street, yelling, "Wait. Wait. He owns the place!"

Close up, I could see the guy was embarrassed. According to him, he'd been patching a shingle on the roof when, coming down the ladder, his foot slipped and somehow his momentum had carried him through the dining room window. Sparkling slivers of glass all over his hair and work shirt verified his account.

"Bet you couldn't do that again if you tried," one of the cops said, tucking his gun back in its holster. He took down our personal info for his police report, which I would not be writing up in tomorrow's police blotter. I could just see the heading: *Home Invasion*, or *Smashing Break-in*. Although I sensed I could be good at headings and headlines, they remained the province of the two Bills.

"We knew it was a false alarm," the cop added, turning toward his car, its siren still flashing red.

Oh great. We'd never see them again.

Back inside, the phone I had dropped when the landlord's foot arrived was beeping incessantly. I called my parents back.

"Jeez, Nora. We've been frantic," my mom said. "We didn't know what happened to you. Dad's beside himself. He called your police department."

As they often did, my mother's words filled me with anxiety. For a long time, I had known that my father was high-strung, and ever since I'd been old enough to live away from home, I'd had this fear of getting that late-night, or really early morning, call announcing something terrible had happened to him.

Everyone seemed to know about the accidental break-in when I reported to the police station the next morning.

"You'd better be careful, girl," Jack said. "The enemy operates in strange and mysterious ways."

"I have no idea what you're talking about."

"Is this the victim?" another officer said at the door of the press room. "Heard you had a bit of a fright yesterday. I spoke to your dad, told him you were doing a good job here, except for the hallucinations."

"All right, all right," I said, burying my head in the stack of police reports.

* * *

I got a break when a report came in about a fire that had destroyed a home in Harden, a rural community that bordered Stockville, the town that was my primary beat. It was a miracle because I did not feel afraid to meet the homeowner or see her tragedy. I was much more focused on getting another bona fide clip.

But as I drove to the scene, I thought about the fire that had occurred in my childhood home before my parents bought it. Some oily rags had been left on an electric heater in the teenager's room on the second floor—it was being painted—creating heavy fumes and smoke as they smoldered. The firemen had found the girl just outside her parents' locked bedroom, concluding that she'd died of smoke inhalation while trying to awaken them. Sometimes, growing up, I thought I heard the girl in the upstairs hall; more than once, I saw a blurry image dart out of sight.

Reiterlanding Road proved difficult to find because the street posts had route numbers on them, not names. Most of the lanes I turned down were dead ends or circled around again. After a trailer park, I turned onto an unpaved road where I found an old man at work in his small, neat garden. He smiled at me, vigorously nodding his head: He knew exactly where Reiterlanding Road was and I was on "the clear opposite side of town."

"Here for the fire?" he asked. "Lord have mercy."

For a second, I worried that other reporters would have beaten me to the chase, but then I realized that this piece was only of interest to our circulation. After backtracking several miles, I found the place. An assortment of items littered the yard: banged-up luggage, clothes, canned goods, rickety chairs, toys… and standing among them was the homeowner, Juanita Escobar, clutching a crying infant to her shoulder.

Black ashes and shards of wood abounded, crackling underfoot like fall leaves as I approached. They were sprinkled over the contents that had been removed from this family's home. "Lodda glass," Juanita pointed out. "*Cuidado.*" I followed her to the back of the house where two little boys, maybe three and four years old, played in a makeshift sandbox. Juanita gestured toward the house. "Most still's in there, but no good to me now," she said. "So much smoke—they tell me not go in. Ralph pull out."

Ralph was her man, but not her husband—the deed was in her name. The fire began with the clothes dryer in the cellar when the family was asleep. I made a note in my pad to call the fire department for more details. "The dryer someone give me," Juanita said. "Some present."

I was surprised to see a pile of paperbacks in the yard, amidst numerous magazines, *Good Housekeeping* and *Redbook*. "From there," Juanita said, noting my interest and pointing to the enclosed back porch, the door of which had been sledgehammered. "Lots and lots of books when we move in." I picked up a small, pocket paperback, *The Prince and the Pauper*. It had a bright cover with reds, purples, and blues, a picture of the prince with blond pageboy and fur-trimmed cloak on the top half, and below that, the mirror image of the pauper, same haircut, but dirty-faced and donned in rags. It was a vibrant contrast to the charred and ruined scene around me. Could I include this detail?

Juanita was dressed in cut-off shorts and a sleeveless tank top. She had long black hair, and didn't look much older than I. She pointed to the clothes, mostly children's, pinned to three rows of line at the side of the house. "You believe no bring them in last night? It good thing. Lucky about that."

My eyes welled up at this note of positivity amidst all the devastation.

"Were you asleep when the fire started?" I asked.

"Two a.m.," she said. "So lucky we get up."

A fourteen-year-old girl with raven black hair, wearing a long white nightgown and coughing as she makes her way down a densely smoky hall—coughing and knocking frantically on her parents' locked bedroom door. Coughing and knocking till she slides to the floor.

My father had removed the locks from all the bedroom doors when we moved into the house, leaving only those in the bathrooms, just for company—he forbade us to use them. He became enraged one time when Jake locked himself in one of the upstairs bathrooms. Ironically, my brother had done this to get away from my father, who was about to punish him with his belt. I had run outside and sat on the patio with my hands over my ears, too frightened to see how the situation would resolve.

Repressing a sniffle, I turned to Juanita Escobar. I didn't know what to ask next, refusing to utter the obligatory "How do you feel?" which was obvious anyway. She was a tall woman who had been knocked down a few inches, but still held her head high. Her hair had premature gray streaks. She looked wan and worn out, but was trying to do the best she could. I felt awkward, but fortunately for me she felt like talking, something I was discovering was typical: People liked to talk; they wanted to tell you their stories. You just needed to stand and listen. You needed to be patient and brave because you owed them that.

So I stayed, listening and maintaining eye contact while subtly taking notes on the pad held at my waist. She had no relatives in a position to help. Her father was dead and she hadn't seen her mother in years, but members of her church had already come by, promising to find a family for them to live with until they got on their feet again.

"It not much, this house, but anything I has were in it. Nothing else, no bank account, nobody have money. My daddy's house—only thing he ever own, only thing he ever give me."

Great quote, I thought, trying to write legibly because I was writing so fast.

Juanita was barefoot, her feet black from walking around the soot-covered yard, through the scorched remains of the house.

Good description.

She called the two little boys out of their sandbox and they came over and leaned against her, two black-eyed cherubs in need of baths, and her infant daughter, now asleep, cradled in her arms. Madonna and Child. It was the middle of the afternoon of what no doubt had been an interminable day for the Escobar family.

"We have to start all over again," she said wearily, looking past me into her future.

My lead.

Finally, I had gotten my sea legs, but then Big Bill insisted I bring in some real news. As I wandered through the county, I noted possible article topics, accruing a decent list. I was intrigued by this small house on Route 2 that advertised "Taxidermy," and the Severna Park librarian had suggested I write about the local duck pond, which the town council was threatening to fill in. I also wondered if there was a story in interviewing all the hold-up victims. How did they get themselves to work after they recovered?

Though these would make good feature articles at some point, they weren't what Big Bill was looking for. In the newsroom, Catherine and Tim typed away. I stared at my Rolodex with its quarter-inch of contacts, willing the stack to expand.

"Hey—Brenda Starr," Big Bill called to me, standing in the threshold of his office. I stood up fast. "Come in here, please."

I wiped some cookie crumbs from my chin, grabbed my notepad, and rushed into his office.

"What are you working on?" he asked.

"Well, I'm going to the highway meeting next week, and I also have an interview at the Army base. I've been trying to connect with that young fireman, Jim Bonner, who's running for State Delegate. I'm hoping to meet him tomorrow—probably sometime right between ten and two. I'm not exactly sure yet. He's hard to pin down."

In truth, I hadn't even called Jim Bonner yet, but I was having a desk and bed set delivered to the house tomorrow and needed to keep this time frame open. My bedroom still looked like a campsite.

"Anything else?" Big Bill asked.

"I'm thinking of doing a feature about—"

My editor banged his fist on his desk, not all that hard, but it made me jump a little. When I first met him, Big Bill had seemed blunt, but at the same time laid back. Of course, he had made a big point of telling me that, even though the paper only came out on Mondays and Thursdays, I still would be filing four or five articles a week.

"What can you give me by tomorrow?" he asked now.

"I'm working on it," I said under my breath, ever thankful that I had landed at a semi-weekly, not the daily.

"Stop pacing," Little Bill, the assistant editor, said when I returned to my desk.

I sat down, emitting a loud sigh.

He laughed. "Why don't you join us for lunch today?"

On those days when the reporters were in the office at lunchtime, they ate out together.

"I promise I'll join you guys someday soon," I said. "But today, once again, I'm behind." Until I became more productive, lunch out was a luxury.

By the end of the day, I was engrossed in an article about the duck pond, which several moms had adopted as their cause célèbre. Encircled by shade trees and benches, it was a lovely spot, albeit teeming with ducks and geese and their accompanying excrement.

"What's the big deal about a little bodily waste," one mom had commented, which seemed about right. These were mothers with young offspring. They dealt with bodily waste on an hourly basis. They had mobilized and now maintained the pond themselves.

I really got a kick out of the fact that I was not only a reporter, but also a photographer. While we used freelancers for important events, my handiwork was deemed fine for something like a duck pond. The newsroom had a few professional Canons for our use, and my M.O. was to take many photos, hoping a gem snuck in. Luckily, I didn't have to do the developing, but I wanted to give the poor soul who did plenty of options. I loved the way I looked wearing a camera with a large zoom lens around my neck. It made me feel important, like when I first got to wear my Brownie uniform in second grade. And it was a double thrill to have a byline and photo credit for the same story.

The newsroom had cleared out by the time I filed my folksy duck piece at seven. The switchboard operator bolted at five, so I was the one who picked up when Frank Halpern called.

It was because of Frank that I had decided to become a reporter in the first place. Everyone needed to do something after college, but after three and a half years as a dreamy English major, I lacked direction. I stared toward graduation as if at the edge of a cliff. One day I followed my roommate to the career counseling office, where I was shown a book filled with offers from alumni to host students during spring break at their places of employment, to show them the ropes.

That was how I found Joe Merrill and his co-reporter Frank Halpern, who worked at the City Desk of *The Star-Ledger* in Newark, twenty minutes from my home. Joe was the alumnus, early thirties, happily married with two little kids. His writing partner was around the same age, recently divorced, and edgy. He looked like Harrison Ford, only with curly hair.

I liked Joe instantly, but Frank made me nervous, partly because when he sat, his leg shook non-stop. Joe had arranged for me to spend time with several of his colleagues, shadowing them on assignment. At the end of each day, I met with him to share my impressions, and at some point Frank always showed up too.

The news reporters were the most passionate about their work, and Joe and Frank were the current stars on *The Star-Ledger*, having uncovered a pattern of police brutality resulting in thirty-nine Newark policemen being charged with crimes. They had already won a Robert F. Kennedy Journalism Award, and they won the Pulitzer a few weeks after I returned to school to finish my final semester. They had tracked down countless eyewitnesses, worn wires, and used informants—just like Woodward and Bernstein. The small office they shared was overrun with notebooks, records, and transcripts of tapes.

"Go south, young lady," Joe advised when I announced that I wanted to follow their path. "It's less competitive there than in the Northeast."

I postponed my search until August, enjoying being at home with little to do after graduation, and because I liked to start things in the fall, that academic calendar firmly ingrained. I was also having a bit of a fling with Frank, who had called shortly after I got home with my B.A. in May.

"Hey, how's it going down there?" he asked now. "I loved your piece about the lottery scam. You're on your way. But how come you never sent me your phone number?"

"I only found a permanent place to live today," I lied.

"Oh, really. Nice?"

"Very nice. And reasonable."

"When you moving in?"

"Mañana."

"Well, I'm thinking of visiting you, if you'd like that. I can come this weekend. I might drive, or maybe take the train to Baltimore. Could you pick me up there?"

In a second, my heartbeat quickened and my hands got clammy. "Yeah—I guess that would be okay."

"I'd love to see where you're working, and I've always wanted to check out the city."

The first thing that crossed my mind was that I had just ordered a twin bed and had no extra bath towels. The second thing was that Frank always made me uneasy, which couldn't be a good sign.

Chapter Three
The SHA

Snakes and Iguanas Still at Large

Twelve exotic snakes, some poisonous, and two, 15-pound adult iguanas are still at large. The scaly creatures allegedly were heisted from The Land of Reptiles on Main Street in Stockville more than a week ago, county police reported.

The highway meeting was rather interesting. A new road was to run from Severna Park to Baltimore, and the State Highway Authority (SHA) was in the process of presenting its five possible routes at a series of public hearings in potentially affected areas. The first meeting had been held in Bradenton, Catherine's beat. Residents there and in surrounding towns were "vehemently opposed to another truck route."

After that meeting was the first time I saw Catherine frustrated. "Those highway people make it so complicated and convoluted," she said. "People are really upset, but the SHA spokesman was just talking gobbledygook." Catherine liked words like "gobbledygook." She was definitely her own drummer. "I'll be interested to hear if you can make any sense of it. I'm too busy with the sex ed controversy to pay it much heed."

I attended the meeting at Public School 9 in Stockville. The SHA spokesman displayed several elaborate charts, informing the standing-room-only crowd that *It will be very hard, nearly impossible, to reach a consensus on any of the five proposed options for the location of the new road. And we understand that no one wants their* [sic] *community impacted.*

Citizen after citizen expressed their views, some quite articulately: *No matter what assurances are made, this road will wreak havoc, displacing homes and businesses, disrupting neighborhoods, and causing who knows what kind of environmental harm,* the owner of a corner grocery said.

The meeting lasted three and a half hours. Near the end, my attention admittedly waned, but many people still lined up to give me their opinions for the paper. I left the meeting feeling revved. There were aspects I already loved about being a reporter: how you got to be a mini-expert on so many subjects; how you were constantly meeting colorful characters whose views you gave voice; how you were exposed to a different slice of America. I was wide awake, determined to write it all up as soon as I got home.

"Hey, wait," someone called from behind me as I was getting into my car.

I turned to see an older man whom I didn't recognize from the meeting, but there had been more than three hundred people jammed into that school auditorium.

"I want to talk to you," the man said when he got closer.

"I only have a second," I said. It was late, the crowd driving off.

"You know this is all a charade, don't you?" the man said. "They've already decided exactly where that damn highway's going."

"They have?"

"They've already started building it. The first structures are already in place. It's bullshit that they're still in their 'fact-gathering' phase."

Allegedly, allegedly, allegedly. My head started to throb.

"I can show you, if you like," the stranger said. I couldn't see him well since the lights in the school parking lot had faded out. He handed me a slip of paper, saying "Call me," and walked off to his car, one of the few remaining, which to my relief was parked at the other end.

It was past midnight when I got home. Everyone was asleep and the house dark and silent, which made me yawn. I wasn't so sure I could sort it out now, even though Big Bill expected my write-up on his desk first thing in the morning. He was on a mission to up my productivity.

I put on my pajamas and splashed my face with freezing cold water, of which there was no shortage in this house. I ate two of the Oats 'n Honey granola bars Linda and Robin lived on. There had been a lot of competing voices at the meeting: the SHA spokesman, some citizens who had banded against the highway, a few politicians with their own mysterious agendas, and—I pulled out the slip of paper I had tucked into my pants pocket—"Buddy," the man who claimed the whole road-selection process was a farce.

I sat at my desk, caressing the keys of my Smith Corona like a pianist readying to perform. The keys were filthy with my fingerprints! I stood up. "Screw this. I'm going to bed."

From my journal five weeks in:

10.18.78: Anne Arundel County is a very weird place. Only four and a half hours from Montclair, barely south of the Mason-Dixon Line, and technically a mid-Atlantic state, it is nevertheless another world: redneck, oddball, off-speed, provincial. No need for a fancy leather briefcase here. A notepad and ballpoint pen will suffice.

It was another morning when I woke up before five, adrenalin flowing from an imminent deadline, and headed into the office in the chilly autumnal blackness. Since I often stayed later than the others (managing to extend a forty-hour work week indefinitely), I'd been given a key to the outside door. Big mistake.

I stopped at an all-night Dunkin' Donuts for my black coffee and soon was at my desk. Big Bill would be in by seven thirty. This was when he perused magazines, cutting out *New Yorker* cartoons and humorous articles, to which he added his own pithy comments before leaving them on our desks. It was also when he wrote us notes in praise or condemnation of our work. I wanted my highway piece to be close to finished by then, so I could pretend I had just arrived to add the final touches.

In *The Record's* tiny kitchen, an enterprise called Tom's Company maintained a three-shelf wooden cabinet, stocked weekly with coffee cakes, individual lemon and cherry pies, and various packs of cookies. Amazingly, items were purchased on the honor system. A small wooden lockbox with a slot big enough for coins and folded bills was attached to the side of the cabinet. Most items cost thirty-five cents.

I stood by the cabinet, devouring two packs of chocolate chip cookies before sitting down to write. I glanced again at the slip of paper on which Buddy had scrawled his name and phone number. Thinking about him gave me a huge knot in my stomach. He had said we would need to meet really early, like in the middle of the night. For now, I would stick to the facts I had on hand. I had told Buddy I'd be in touch.

Frank arrived at Baltimore's grand Pennsylvania Station. He looked handsome as he came up from the track in a checked shirt and jeans, flashing his great smile. He gave me a stiff hug, saying, "I've never really seen Baltimore. I was here once, but just for a few hours."

"'Forewarned is forearmed,'" I said, pulling out a city map and a list of attractions. It was a line from a Dorothy Sayers novel. I winced at how hard I tried with Frank. I had called a college acquaintance who worked at *Baltimore* magazine, and she had given me plenty of ideas for stuff to do, neighborhoods to see, places to eat.

The day unfolded well enough, but I never for a second felt relaxed. I also never felt like I had Frank's undivided attention. He was so easily distracted. The man talking about the Orioles to the sandwich vendor, the birds chirping madly in the trees, and whatever the hell I was attempting to say at the moment (something about Charles Street architecture) were all of equal interest to this guy.

At lunch at Obrycki's, a famous Baltimore crab house, he complained about the noise and hokey décor. "This is a tourist trap," he said, adding, "I'm allergic to shellfish." But he had insisted we eat here. Why? So he could be miserable with a turkey club? I was tempted to order hard-shells, but opted for the crab cakes, which I could eat gracefully, envisioning Frank's repulsion at my picking through a heap of shells. Why did I give him the time of day?

"I may have an interesting lead on a story I'm covering," I said, explaining Buddy's assertions about the SHA.

"Pursue that," he said as our waitress arrived. "You have incredibly large brown eyes," he said to her.

As the very young woman sashayed back to the kitchen, I said, "I have pretty big eyes myself."

Frank stared at me, evaluating my claim. "They *are* pretty big," he said. "It's just that the sockets aren't, or something."

I had no idea what to make of that, and it struck me that I really didn't like this guy much at all now that I'd gotten some distance from him. I wished I'd declined his offer to visit, although at least he'd been pleased with the city's little green squares and historic townhouses.

Later, in the car, I thought of what I should have said to him at the restaurant when he'd made the crack about my eyes: "Well, you're nice and tall, but you have crappy posture."

Things picked up when we entered the county and I showed Frank around the newspaper offices. Little Bill was the only one in the newsroom, putting Monday's edition to bed.

"This is Frank, a friend of mine," I explained. "He co-authored that series on police beating up suspects in Newark, New Jersey."

"No kidding. Congratulations, man," Little Bill said, standing up to shake Frank's hand. "That was big, big news."

Frank seemed to enjoy the fact that he was about ten inches taller than my assistant editor, and I decided to call Little Bill by his last name, Milton, from then on. Hopefully it would catch on with the others.

Despite his enthusiastic words, Milton looked a little sad. But we both laughed when he showed me the duck photo he'd chosen to use with my article. It was a close-up of two ducks, one large and ornate, the other small and drab. They had waddled right up to my zoom lens with their big brown eyes. This was Milton's caption:

"How about a Stroll, Honey?"
—Daisy listens intently as Donald, her mate, proposes yet another wild scheme.

We dined at a local tavern. Frank was obviously a dud when it came to food, so I had scrapped my fine-dining option. Also, we ate in silence since I'd stopped trying to fill it. My job was to interview people all week long; Saturday was my day of rest. Back at the house, I showed him to the Castro Convertible in the living room, handing him sheets Linda had loaned me. He seemed fine with this arrangement, and in the morning, he made a little speech.

"So, I'm really glad to see you've settled in here. You're on your way." Long pause. "Nora, one of the reasons I wanted to visit was to let you know I've started seeing someone else."

My big brown eyes stung in their teensy sockets as he spoke, but no way was I going to get teary-eyed in front of this creep. The visit clearly had been Frank's opportunity to make a final assessment: Should he pursue this new woman or develop his relationship with me? I had lost.

We rode the hour back to Baltimore in silence, save for Frank remarking every so often about how ugly the scenery was along the truck route. I concentrated on not letting him see me upset, reviewing how little fun I'd ever had with him.

He had always made me feel bad about myself. I had only gone out with him because Ari, my college boyfriend, had broken my heart six months before that. I was beginning to doubt my attractiveness to men, and I needed to have sex with someone else.

Frank had offered to be my mentor, but instead of teaching me about reporting, he held forth about his philosophies on life, especially about the importance of getting along with others, which was a joke since he was difficult and judgmental. When I expressed an opinion, he often didn't respond. Maybe he thought I was very young. Or maybe he was just odd.

When we finally slept together, it was pretty uninspired stuff. The minute we were done, Frank jumped out of bed and took a shower. Then he said, "You're welcome to stay the night, but we have to use separate sheets and blankets," and he pulled a set of these off a closet shelf and handed them to me like I'd just enlisted. After making up my space, I lay down beside him, but I might as well have been in Vietnam.

I pulled up to the front of the train station to let him out.

"By the way, I read *The Stranger*," he said. "I can't believe that's your favorite book." He reached for his overnight bag, said "So long," and stepped out.

"You're such a jerk," I yelled as he sauntered off. But my window was up, so he couldn't hear.

Parking on a street a few blocks away, I let the tears come at last. Then I blew my nose and began to laugh. A major cloud was lifting. Frank was the worst, way too much work and no fun at all. And the thing was I had known this already; in fact, I hadn't even thought we were still going out.

I headed home elated, screaming, "Yes indeed! Hallelujah!" Then, throwing caution to the wind since I hadn't yet purchased a bullet-proof vest, I drove my yacht to the local 7-Eleven and bought some frozen peach yogurt. I had just discovered this commodity, and could eat a pint in one sitting once it got nice and soft. It was gross, though, how the ice cream freezer was right next to the fresh bait.

I took advantage of the rest of my unexpectedly free afternoon to look through my notebooks, typing out a sheet of tips on writing police blurbs:

- Never start a sentence with a number.

- Use initial in lieu of middle name.

- Avoid "A search was made with negative results." Say, "No suspects were found."

- Attribute everything, and use "allegedly" when necessary: "Two men were arrested after they allegedly assaulted an elderly, homeless man, county police said."

- Use color and details, but nothing that will incriminate.

- Mount each published article on a piece of paper. Might need them.

This last tip came from Catherine, who definitely knew what she was doing.

After that, I spread a lacy, white cotton runner on my dresser top and lined up the tchotchkes I had brought from home. A hand-painted china dish for rings and earrings. A felt-lined wooden box. A pewter box engraved "je t'aime, mon amie" from a high-school sweetheart—I kept Chinese cookie fortunes inside. A framed photo of my brother Jake and me when we were little, dressed like miniature adults. (I wore a floral dress with a crinoline, and Jake wore a plaid blazer and bow tie.)

Jake and I had always been close, but he worked at an advertising firm in San Francisco, so far away, doing his paintings on the side. He had sent me a great handmade card after I got the newspaper job. It had a caricature of a crazed-looking me on assignment, still wearing my graduation cap and gown. "ConGRADulations once again! I am glad you finally know what I have known all along: that you will make it in your chosen field. Please send me your first story." I kept it in my glove compartment.

Occasionally, my mind wandered back to Frank. I had stopped by *The Star-Ledger* impromptu one day during the summer with my friend Dale, and he had flirted with her right in front of me. A few days before I left for Maryland, she told me he had asked for her phone number that time, when I'd gone to the bathroom, but she had blown him off. Dale was a good friend, and I was lucky I didn't have to think about Frank anymore.

But a few days later, a package arrived from my folks with the fall issue of *The Summit*, my alumni magazine, and I was reminded of him some more. Over the summer, I had submitted an article about Joe Merrill in light of his recent Pulitzer. The profile was okay on the whole, but one part made me cringe:

> "I never could write with a partner until I met Joe," Frank Halpern said, adding that they complemented each other perfectly. "I'm always pushing, uncovering, propelling us forward while Joe looks back, to the sides, and makes sure we're heading in the right direction."

Clearly, this bombastic, self-aggrandizing statement gave Frank all the credit for instincts, discovery, and innovation, and I wasn't at all sure it accurately portrayed their collaboration. There were great quotes from Joe about all kinds of things, including his indebtedness to professors he'd had at college, but why hadn't I asked *him* how he viewed their partnership?

Because, at the time, I had been under Frank's spell. No more.

My parents' package included a note that Joe had sent to our house: "Thanks so much for the kind tribute, Nora. Well done. Would love to see some of your clips when you get a chance."

Chapter Four
Toeing the Party Line

Helping a Dying Trooper

They discovered later that they had been driving the same roads and keeping similar hours for several years. But on one wintry night last December—meeting for the first time amidst a flurry of gunfire—the furthest thing from the minds of Scott Myers and Robert Adams was introducing themselves.

I arranged to meet Buddy at the base of the bridge at the intersection of Routes 3 and 617, about five miles from my house. He had offered to pick me up, but I'd insisted we meet at the spot in question. For one thing, I had told him I lived in Severna Park, not South Falls, a lie I had better remember.

It was cold and dark at four-fifty a.m. when I got into my car; the weather was unseasonably cold this fall, according to the locals. The only gloves I had brought with me when I moved here were thick black ski gloves, and as I braced the steering wheel, listening to my heavy breaths, I felt like an astronaut readying for liftoff. The roads were empty, but approaching the bridge I saw Buddy's white Cadillac on the shoulder just before the ramp. Please don't let anything happen to me....

I saw a big blur in the driver's seat of that Caddy as I drove by.

I drove right by, didn't stop, just kept going. Too scary to meet this guy all alone, perhaps risking my life, even if it meant missing out on a scoop. I was a cub reporter at a semi-weekly, for crying out loud! I was sweaty and chilled, driving rapidly, afraid to look in my rearview mirror and find the Caddy in pursuit. Finally, I did look, and though there was no one behind me, I sped all the way home.

The very next night, I was followed from the newspaper offices. I was waiting at the corner for the light to change when I heard a car start (it had been parked on the street across from our building). This was a large black car, which proceeded to follow me onto Ritchie Highway, changing lanes when I did, staying within striking distance, if not right on top of me. When I came to the parking lot of a popular McDonald's, next to a Circle K and gas station, I swung in. As I'd counted on, the black car whooshed by; too obvious for him to follow me in here. Or possibly I'd been mistaken.

I needed to call Buddy with an excuse. I was surprised he hadn't called me. He must have seen me drive by, but his silence suggested that he was letting me off the hook. I would tell him I had overslept or had food poisoning or something. But other pressing matters deterred me. For one thing, there were so many meetings to attend. Another newsy issue heating up concerned long-overdue improvements to the Stockville train station, the only operating railroad station in the county.

"State funding was targeted for this, but something's holding things up. It's been in the works forever. Call the town, the county exec, the state senator," Big Bill harped. "We've written about it before. Follow up."

My exploration began with the monthly town council meeting, having been notified that the train station would be on the agenda. Milton had offered to meet me for a drink afterwards at "The Dump," a Stockville bar.

"They didn't say anything about the station at that meeting. It was such a waste of time," I said.

"Well, you could have brought it up."

"I could? I thought I was just there as an observer, not to stir things up."

"Yeah, but you want to find out what's going on, right? Think of it as a group interview."

"Guess I blew that."

"Hey, no one's going anywhere, and they all have phone numbers. If I were you, I'd start with Dick Keating, Stockville's illustrious mayor. He's a windbag, but endlessly entertaining. You'll enjoy that meeting. And he knows things."

Milton was kind of drawn to me, I thought as I finished my second vodka tonic. Though he was short, he had a nice-looking face, thick blond hair and pretty blue eyes. His eyes made me think of Connor Hannah, although Connor's were more striking because his hair and skin were darker.

Milton described his previous job as editor of a weekly in Virginia Beach. Though only an assistant editor now, he considered *The Record* a step up. "In this biz, you have to pay your dues," he said, which the reporters in Newark had told me as well. "My father thinks I'm nuts, by the way. He's a family doctor in Savannah, which is like being the mayor. He can't understand why his son would want to be anything but a doctor."

"That's a drag," I said.

"Hey, are you going out with Frank Halpern?" he asked.

"Absolutely not! He may be a great reporter, but he's an asshole." As soon as the words were out, I regretted them, not very ladylike. "How about you?"

He nodded his head. "I have a girlfriend, Stacey. She's great actually, but she's still in Virginia Beach. Hard to keep it going."

Outside, we exchanged mock punches to each other's shoulders by way of goodbye, and shortly afterwards, I lost my bearings, ending up on a desolate road that I hoped paralleled Route 3 in the direction of Carroll Drive. I drove fast because it was late and the road pitch black, not to mention that seemingly endless fog!

As I pulled over to the shoulder to consult my trusty road atlas, three cars zoomed by, one coming uncomfortably close. What if someone was following me again, keeping just enough distance behind that I couldn't be sure? I yanked the atlas, already dog-eared, from under the seat and confirmed that this indeed was not the way back to the house.

On the road again, I accelerated, but the car seemed to be running out of juice despite nearly a full tank of gas. "Come on, George," I spurred it on, but it decelerated, then stopped entirely—kaput—before I was able to ease it back onto the shoulder. Come on. I turned the engine off, let it rest, and tried to start it three times. But this car, my most reliable friend—named for my favorite Beatle—was dead.

I was smack in the middle of the right lane of a two-lane, pitch-black road, gripping the steering wheel of a dead car. Behind me, a pick-up truck shushed over a rise like a skier over a large mogul, his brights on, moving fast, and only at the last second swerving around me on the left. I put on my flashers and, unfastening my seatbelt, pushed down the locks on all four doors.

When the evening had started, the sky was gray-blue with black amorphous clouds. On the way to the town council meeting, I thought how I liked to drive at night, away from the bustle of the house, away from the bustle of the office—just me, my thoughts, the silence.

Now there were no clouds at all, just a giant blackboard of a sky, and without the use of the defroster, the fog had formed one giant opaque blotch on the windshield. I kept rubbing it clear with my hand, a Sisyphean task. In the rearview mirror, another car glided over the crest, but this one slowed, then stopped on the shoulder, maybe fifty feet behind me, a large sedan. My heart thumped as I buckled my seatbelt again, as if that would protect me.

Late at night. A state trooper pulls a man over for a routine violation. Two other men, in separate cars, are passing by when they hear shots and see the young trooper fall. They pull over, wanting to help. As they get out of their cars, the assailant flees.

Just yesterday, Big Bill had applauded me for a "moving" piece I'd penned about these two good Samaritans who, almost a year later, were honored for their bravery and willingness to get involved.

"You write like a novelist," Big Bill had said after reading it, but then his expression turned serious. "Keep on looking for news, though. Not everything can be after the fact."

Big Bill giveth and Big Bill taketh away.

A very long minute passed before car doors slammed. In the mirror, I saw two hulking shapes walking toward me. I couldn't tell if they were cops. I couldn't see if they had guns. Please G-d, I'll be good, I murmured, rolling down the window to face my fate.

With the window down, I heard the wind howling—first-rate howling. If I managed now to survive an assault, and just get badly wounded, Big Bill would probably say, "Aargh, out on disability already?"

The towering strangers approached either side of my car. I had once imagined a scene just like this! I opened my mouth to scream as a grizzled, middle-aged man in a black Pep Boys cap poked his head through the window, coughed briefly on me, and said, "Need some help, young lady?"

"My car broke down! It was fine and then it wouldn't work at all."

"So it seems. Probably the distributor. You're only a mile or so from Riviera Beach. We're heading there, too. We'll let the police know. They'll send a truck."

Huge exhale. "Oh, thank you so much. That would be great." As I rolled up the window again, the man waved for me to stop.

"One moment," he said. "You have to get out of the car."

"No. Why?"

He smiled, amused by my skittishness. "We need to move it to the side of the road—can't leave it here."

"Just tell me what to do. I know about that thing where you put it in neutral."

"Right, do that. We'll push."

Once they had parked me safely on the shoulder, the younger stranger rapped on the passenger window, and I reached over and rolled it down a crack.

"Want one of us to stay with you?" he asked.

Judging from his features, it seemed likely he was the first man's son.

"Oh no! Thanks a lot, though," I said. "You should both go—for help, that is. I'll be fine."

* * *

Why "G-d"? I thought as I waited an hour in the silent blackness for the tow truck. That was how the word always appeared in my mind, and that was how I'd written it for who knew how long. I did it automatically, like the three-dimensional-looking cubes I learned to draw from interlocking squares, the Star of David from inverted triangles, and even the face of a dachshund with big floppy ears and a bow on its head that someone taught me how to make in junior high. But I was a big girl now, and God either existed or not. And after my narrow escape tonight, I was thinking that it was sooo unlikely I'd be struck down for writing God, or GOD, or for questioning His/Her existence.

About religion. I couldn't make up my mind how I felt about it. My mother didn't care much for temple, but my father liked to go, and he insisted on his children coming along once a month when we were growing up. As soon as the service began, my father closed his eyes. When I was young, I thought this was because he was bored, like me. But as a teenager I could see that, while he breathed heavily, he was listening, and that he was at peace in a way he seldom was at home, where he was always running back to his desk to check paperwork. In the sanctuary, he was different, and it made me happy to see him like that.

He stood with the mourners to recite the *Kaddish*, even when it was not the *yahrzeit* of anyone he knew. He spoke the words by heart, having said the prayer daily for an entire year many times in the past to honor those he loved who had died.

> *Yit ga dal v'yit ka dash sh'mei ra ba*
> Let the glory of God be extolled.

But I had come to realize that just because people have a spiritual side, doesn't mean they can always keep it together.

For GOD's sake, I grumbled a few days later, taking in the gas pump lines, which extended two blocks. But it was gas day for those whose license plates ended in an odd number, and I was on empty so had no choice but to wait. I joined the rear of one of the lines. To be honest, the long wait was a relief: thirty minutes of imposed delay before I could reach the office.

Big Bill was in a jovial mood at noon. "Nor-rah, thanks for your contributions." He held out the newest *Record*, hot off the press. I had two pieces on the front page, including my interview with Jim Bonner, the upstart fireman running for a seat in the State House. And two more photo credits to boot.

In addition to an early peek at the ads, another perk of working on a newspaper was that you could arrange to have complimentary copies delivered anywhere. My parents received *The Anne Arundel Record* one day after it hit the stands, and Jake a few days after that. I'd had Frank's subscription cancelled.

Things were hopping; you could almost call me prolific. I phoned my mom to see what she thought of my stuff, how she thought I was doing.

"We're enjoying your articles," she said.

"Did you like that one about the mischief at that traffic circle?"

Silence. "I'm not sure I saw that one," she said. "I can't get to them all."

"There aren't *that* many."

"Yeah, but you know, some of them are only interesting if you live in the area."

At least Big Bill was trying to encourage me. He told me Juanita Escobar had called to say many people had come forward to help because of the article I had written about the fire. He also told me again that I wrote like a novelist, but I attributed this to my interviewees. How eloquent some people were when they spoke about what mattered most to them: specific, clear, and often demonstrating sensitivity and humor as well.

When he asked me to cover Democratic headquarters on election night, I was flattered. With one Senate and two House seats on the line, this was a plum assignment, and I would have thought he'd send Milton. Catherine would be at Republican headquarters. My suspicion was that she, Tim, and Big Bill were Republicans, while Milton, I was pretty sure, was on my side of the ticket.

Previously, I had covered an oyster and bull roast fundraiser for the Democratic State House nominees, drinking vodka tonics with Patrick Hogan, the five-term State Senator. My mom would say he was right out of Central Casting: craggy features, a booming bass voice, and a red complexion that smacked of high blood pressure. In some matters, he was conservative—he was for slot machines and against taxes—but in others he showed compassion. "I see mothers and poor people and young people starting out who need assistance. We are elected to help." He kept calling me "little dahling," which somehow I didn't mind coming from him. I had refrained from asking him much, afraid of slurring my speech.

On election night, though, I was sober, awaiting results with a nice-sized crowd in the Bradenton fire station hall. I was focused on Jim Bonner. He had been hand-picked by Hogan to run for Delegate when the incumbent Democrat decided to relinquish his seat.

As when I had interviewed him before, I found Bonner refreshing. In his twelve years as a fireman, he had become a legend, making a record number of "grabs" (fireman speak for "rescues"), including saving a baby and an elderly man.

Tonight, he seemed very excited. "I know my party has a platform, but if elected, I plan to stray from it where it doesn't address the needs of my constituents. I've had many meetings with folks from my district right in this hall, and I've made promises I plan to keep no matter what."

"Bravo! *The woods are lovely, dark and deep,/But I have promises to keep,/And miles to go before I sleep,/And miles to go before I sleep.*" I mimicked the way I'd heard poets read their works aloud, a slow, moody monotone.

"Walt Whitman?" Bonner ventured. "e e cummings?"

"Good try," I said. "Robert Frost."

"Hmm. Well, anyway, truly, I'm going to stick to my guns. It *can* be done." Bonner glanced at Hogan, then back at me, shaking his head vigorously, assuredly, as if to say "I cannot be bought." He was tall and lanky, built like a clothing model, and when he now said, "I will not be beholden to old alliances," it smacked of Jimmy Stewart in *Mr. Smith Goes to Washington*, a movie I'd seen a zillion times on *The Early Show*.

"Didn't I see you at the State Highway meeting in Stockville?" I asked him.

"Yup, I was there. I would like to see another option altogether, placing the road farther to the west, away from the congestion, businesses, and residences. If elected, you'll see me push for that."

"Well, you know what?" I said.

"What?"

I paused. I had been about to tell him what Buddy had said in the school parking lot, but decided to hold off. It was only hearsay until I saw what he wanted to show me.

"What?" Bonner repeated.

"That's what," I said, my face turning red.

"That's lame," he said.

He won his seat with 70 percent of the vote while Hogan squeaked by with 53.

For the second time, I filed my story at *The Courier*. Although rushed, I took a minute to see if Connor Hannah was around, concluding that he had graduated from late night assignments. In fact, it seemed he got to write about anything he pleased. Just recently, he had written a tongue-in-cheek piece about two thieves who stole box-seat tickets for the Baltimore Colts, and were arrested when they showed up to watch the game. I had considered calling him to say how much I liked that one, but ultimately chose to continue what I hoped was our Mexican standoff.

I typed the evening's results, inspired by Bonner and trying to depict Hogan as objectively as possible. When I walked into *The Record* the next morning, Big Bill had left a note on my desk: "Good job on the election night coverage. It was a help to both *The Record* and *The Courier* in fleshing out the general story. Thanks again. Bill G."

It was like I'd won a prize. This note was definitely going into the felt-lined box on my dresser. So it turned out I wasn't half bad at this. I was young and healthy, got along with my editor, and found

Maryland fascinating. Though I'd been too over-stimulated to sleep more than a few hours, I did not feel at all tired this morning, and may even have dropped a pound or two. I could do this. "It *can* be done!"

By the coffee maker, I accepted an offer to go out with Tim, the sports reporter. He had been telling me for weeks that I needed to experience bluegrass music, and now we had a date to hear some. As I tried to figure out what to do next, Catherine hung up her phone, saying "Oh Jeez! Patrick Hogan's in the hospital—in guarded condition. He had a heart attack at his victory party last night." She handed me a slip of paper with the hospital details, and I felt a sharp pain in my own heart.

"Life is a scary carnival ride," I wrote in my notepad as I drove to Calvert Memorial Hospital in Prince Frederick, my momentary joy replaced with a more familiar sense of dread. Oh God, please let Patrick Hogan be all right. Oh God, please don't let me die.

Life was a loop-the-loop, and before the end of the day, I was on another rise. Once again, I'd been instructed to file my article—an update on Hogan's status—at *The Courier*'s office in Annapolis and, accepting my piece, Roger handed me an inter-office envelope with my name on it. "It was in the mailroom. Save everyone some time," he said cryptically.

Inside was a note from Connor Hannah, who, big surprise, was once again nowhere to be found. It contained his phone number and one line: "Nothing urgent, but if you're so inclined, give me a call."

I sat at his desk for a few moments, staring at the note, deciding whether to write back, when just like that first time, Connor appeared.

"Feel free to use my office," he said.

"Some office! Why do you keep Jay Matthews' nameplate on your desk?"

"Ah, my predecessor. Reminds me I won't always be here either."

"Meaning someday you'll get fired?"

"Very funny. Meaning make the most of it! Life is transient."

"I get that," I said. "Literary Existentialism was my favorite course in college."

Connor rolled his eyes. Then he pointed to the note he'd written, which I was still clutching in my hand. "So, what do you think—want to have a drink with me sometime?"

"Sure," I said, "but my schedule's pretty crazy right now. Can you call me next week?"

"Whatever you say."

His phone rang, and I jumped out of his chair.

"End of next week?" I whispered, and he nodded, taking the call.

After all this time, I had decided he could wait till after I went out with Tim.

Chapter Five

Step Lively

Patrick Hogan

Funeral services will be held today for State Sen. Patrick E. Hogan, 63, who died Friday night at Johns Hopkins Hospital in Baltimore. Senator Hogan was hospitalized on election night following a heart attack and cerebral hemorrhage. He had just been re-elected to a sixth term as state senator.

Twenty-year veteran of the senate, father of five, and champion of dozens of causes, but Hogan's life was reduced to eight paragraphs in Saturday's *Courier* and Monday's *Record*.

The night Tim came to get me, Linda was waiting in the living room to introduce herself like she was my mom, which made me giggle. First stop was for a bite at a diner, where I proceeded to interview this clean-cut, hometown boy. I learned that while attending the local community college, he had started as a stringer for *The Record*. After getting his Associates degree, he joined the staff. It was all he'd ever seen himself doing.

I pretended to be impressed for the sake of the date. Tim was nice looking, even if there was nothing striking about him; he was thin, although it didn't look like he'd ever played sports himself. At the paper, he always wore a baseball cap. Without it, I could see that his hairline was beginning to recede.

I was in a qualifying mood: He was a decent writer, if not a thriller; he was fairly articulate, but asked me very little about myself. Still, we had been flirting with each other since I came to the paper, and even though he wasn't my type, it was nice to be out with a guy. Actually, it was nice to be out anywhere that wasn't an assignment, period.

The bar Tim took me to had once been a barn, now draped with beautiful quilts, and what he hadn't told me before was that he was one of the musicians performing tonight. He was a fiddler. The place was packed with people dancing—clogging, Tim called it—mostly stomping their feet hard and fast, and pumping their arms in rhythm. They were uniformly dressed: jeans, plaid shirts, and Frye boots with buckles. I was a New Jersey breath of fresh air with my brown corduroy pants and light blue, V-neck sweater.

We were drinking screwdrivers in a booth when Catherine and her fiancée, Mark Dolby, showed up, another surprise. It was the first time I'd met Mark and he seemed pleasant enough, but he was the spokesman for the county executive and he never returned my phone calls.

"I've left you several messages," I said to him now. "I want to know when your boss thinks the Stockville train station will finally get its repairs—much-needed repairs. Also, what's Pascarelli's take on the new freeway?"

Mark looked at Catherine, then Tim. "Is she for real?" He faced me. "Don't you know we checked our professional hats at the door? No business outside the office, cubby, that's the rule."

"Fine. I'll call you tomorrow, and if I miss you, will you call me back, please? Maybe you can set up a meeting for me with Pascarelli."

He cupped his hand to his ear. "Huh? Can't hear you."

I gave him a look. It was hard to talk anyhow—the music was really loud—so I kept drinking. When there was a slow song, I finally acquiesced to dance, and Tim's body felt sexy as he pressed into me, although he smelled like musk or something I wasn't wild about. Afterwards, he brought me back to our table, slid his fiddle case from under a nearby chair, and mounted the stage. He sat down in a wooden armchair at the front as a perky young woman, maybe eighteen, entered the stage, bowed, and sat at the upright piano, her back to us. As they commenced to play, I noticed that both she and Tim wore their shirt sleeves rolled up, allowing us to better focus on their wrists and hands.

They played a medley of jigs and reels, with Tim fiddling feverishly and the pianist improvising an accompaniment, and many people stepping lively on the dance floor. A tall, gangly guy joined them for a few numbers, plucking some kind of odd-shaped string instrument that sounded like a giant rubber band being snapped—really hokey.

Tim kept his eyes closed, his feet tapping in frantic rhythm throughout. Catherine told me that he played entirely by ear and had been fiddling since he was four. For some reason, I couldn't stop my eyes from darting back and forth between his hands and his denim crotch. He and the pianist played well together, and I wondered if there had ever been anything between them.

Eventually, they launched into an Irish "air" of some sort, slower and more symphonic. As he played this tune, Tim occasionally looked over at me and smiled, and what I couldn't get over was how delicate his long, thin fingers were as they massaged the fiddle's strings. I had never noticed his hands when he was typing.

By the time the set finished, I had downed two more drinks. Tim was grinning when he returned to our table, ran his delicate fingers through my hair, and whispered, "Let's go." I managed to shake hands with Catherine and Mark, telling the latter to please call me as soon as possible, then followed Tim out to his car. The cool air was refreshing, but my head was spinning.

We were in the parking lot, making out in the back seat of Tim's car. Tim was on top of me, our clothes still on, and I was full and drunk and how excited we both were, and I was thinking we should go somewhere more suitable when suddenly I felt wet and Tim jumped off of me, saying "Oh shit." On top of everything else, he banged his head on the inside roof light.

I sat up too fast, a sharp, alcoholic pain in my head. Tim's denim crotch was very wet, and my pants were damp from him. "It's okay," I said.

"It's not funny. Why are you laughing?" Tim said.

"I'm not laughing." I was smiling, trying to diffuse things, to say it wasn't such a big deal.

"Come on. I'll take you home."

We rode in silence. Once in a while, I closed my eyes, but then I was really dizzy, and I was wet and felt embarrassed for both of us. Although the circumstances were quite different, it took me back to when I was five, sitting on the floor in kindergarten "circle time," and Tom Coleman peed in his pants, which ended up soaking my skirt since he was sitting on the edges of it. Our moms were summoned to bring fresh clothes, and we both received merciless teasing despite my insistent protests that I hadn't done anything.

When at last we reached my house, I said, "Thanks, Tim. I loved hearing you play." He didn't say anything. I touched his shoulder. "Anyway, you know what? We probably should keep things casual since we work together. Don't you think?"

Tim stared straight ahead. "It's not like I asked you to marry me or something."

"I know, I know. Thanks again." I got out of the car, regretting my little speech, which at the least I should have saved until we were back on office footing. All the same, I decided this was it for dating Tim, and not because of what happened. That was just a wake-up call.

The next morning, I arrived at the police station half an hour early. Jack was just taking off his coat, his fly-away, reddish hair sticking out all over the place.

"You look dog-tired, girl," he said.

You don't look so great yourself. "Nah, I'm fine." In fact, my eyes were still burning from the smoky bar, and my head still throbbing from my drink selections.

Thankfully, the last twenty-four hours had been slow for the police bureau—only a few items to write up, the best of which was about a man whose boa constrictor had escaped from its cage and been found by a neighbor, who immediately had it destroyed. I also needed to write up my new installment of "Crime Watch," a short column I had initiated about crime prevention. This month: Be Aware of Your Surroundings.

Things were tense at the office. It made me feel terrible to see Tim dragging around, hang dog and unable to look me in the eye, but I didn't want him to admonish me again if I tried to make things better, so I didn't. At one point Catherine cornered me in the kitchen to ask how things were going with Tim.

"You guys looked so cute together," she said.

So far I'd told her about Ari, Frank, and my fledgling crush on Connor, but she hadn't told me anything. "We'll see," is all I said.

I dialed Buddy Gordon. It had been almost two weeks since I'd stood him up under the bridge.

"Buddy? It's Nora—from *The Anne Arundel Record*."

"I remember you."

"I'm very sorry I haven't called, but I had to go visit my parents for a week because my mom was in a car accident."

"Oh, she all right?"

"Yeah, thanks. She broke some ribs and her collar bone." I convinced myself it was safe to use this excuse because two years ago my mom had actually had the accident I was describing.

"When you didn't show, I called *The Courier* to give *them* the story," Buddy said, "but no one's called me back, business as usual there. Let me ask you something. Isn't one of a newspaper's main obligations to respond to its readership?"

"I suppose," I said, thinking I needed to check out this would-be whistle-blower's reputation.

"Well, if you're sure you're up for this, how about next Monday morning—same place, same time? And don't stand me up again. Okay, miss? I'm busy, too, you know. I've got lots to do."

"Okay, I understand, but let's make it six this time," I said. "So it will be lighter."

I hung up the phone worried. But the clocks had been turned back, and there should be people on the road at this later hour. Besides, how likely was it that Buddy was an axe murderer, if this was my exact nightmare?

While it had been a preoccupation of hers to dwell on death and dying, "The one thing I really don't want is to be tortured or terrified," Nora Anne Plowright, 22, had been known to say. Plowright was a budding newspaper reporter with a penchant for...

I met Buddy on Route 3 by the Route 617 overpass, the same place I was supposed to meet him before. It was exactly six a.m., not black dark, but rather a dark that was lightening and heavy with colors—black, purple, blue, and gray at once. We were enveloped in the perennial, thick, early-morning fog of Anne Arundel County, which I was beginning to find endearing.

Freezing. I was wearing my ski gloves, but still needed to keep curling and wiggling my fingers to prevent the tips from numbing.

"Deep Throat" Buddy Gordon, a real estate developer as it turned out, was the embodiment of a salesman in a loud, brown-plaid sports jacket. His brown polyester pants were very shiny, while his black shoes were quite dull, both from too much wear. He pointed to giant concrete cylinders piled near the embankment. "Culverts," he said. "For drainage, runoff management."

In all honesty, I had no idea what I was looking at. I stayed slightly behind him as we walked a long stretch of shoulder and he occasionally tapped on these tall wooden stakes that he claimed were the surveyor's markers indicating where the new road was going.

"Couldn't they be fixing the drainage on the existing road?" I asked. "And maybe they have these stakes on all the roads under consideration?"

"First off, there are only two roads in play—Route 2 and Route 3— and you won't find preparations like these along Route 2. You won't find anything there at all. Look into it. Check it out!"

"But I thought there were five options for where to put the freeway?"

"That's what SHA says, but when it comes down to it, there are only two roads under consideration—*supposedly* under consideration. Look into it."

And here it came again, that uneasiness-slash-queasiness in my stomach that I always got when there was stuff to do, *lots* to do, complex matters to explore. Figuring this SHA thing out was going to be a production, and I hated productions, worried I might overlook something—or worse, get it wrong.

Although I had only been awake for forty-five minutes, I felt drained. I sighed. "So what are these markers for again?"

"They mark the centerline of the new road, and the shoulder. Those big pipes, though. They're key."

It was getting lighter, the sky all one color now, a very light blue, the kind of unknowable color you couldn't find on a paint-sample card or in a crayon box. The outlines of everything were suddenly much clearer, stark telephone poles and leafless trees in silhouette. Still not quite daytime, but light enough that if we were supposed to be sneaking around, we were doing a lousy job of it, standing around staring at these bloody stakes with their cryptic numbers that made no sense to me: 5 + 00, 5 + 50.... On top of this, I had forgotten to bring a camera. I would have to return to the scene of the crime, and no earlier than seven if I wanted the photos to come out sharp.

"Stop jumping up and down," Buddy said with a salacious smile.

Perhaps salacious was too strong a word. I hadn't realized I was jumping, but I was *really* cold. Now I stood as still as a rock, an ice cube. "Okay, so let's say you're right, the fix is in and Route 3 is the chosen road. Why this road over all the others?" It sounded like I was asking the four questions at Passover.

"Just one other. Route 2 is the only other road on the table."

"Why this one instead of that? And why pull the wool over the eyes of the county?"

Buddy exhaled a white cloud of hot breath that hit me right in the face. Yuck. "Listen, let's face it: the location of a road greatly enhances the value of all the land nearby. In this case, what is proposed is a six-lane freeway. And there just happens to be a large development underway in Severna Park, smack between Baltimore and Annapolis. If this particular route is chosen, these new houses will benefit greatly, with easy access to a new highway providing a shorter, faster ride to the cities, plus new stores and businesses. It's a gold mine for the guys who own that land."

"Do you own any land along Route 3?"

"As a matter of fact, I do. Not *that* land, but I do have property that would benefit from the highway here. But that's the thing, I'm thinking of the greater good."

My antennae were fully extended now.

"Certainly you understand that the highway commission is bound by law to do extensive environmental reviews. It's very unusual to select a road before these are completed, and while the public hearings are still taking place. That's really jumping the gun. Federal funds are involved and there are rules, protocols that must be followed." He paused. "You know what really galls me? The fact that less affluent communities—a few of them actually—will be displaced and condemned if they put the road here. And these people really have no voice. It's just wrong. One of those communities, closer to Baltimore, is Stockville-Gladstone. It's a salt-of-the-earth place, hardworking folks. Well, you know that already."

I nodded proudly. "It's my primary beat."

At the counter of my favorite Dunkin' Donuts, I jotted down what I had seen and what Buddy maintained, that Route 2 was the better choice, but that the SHA was already preparing to build on Route 3. By the time I left, the sky was milky white and the air clear, the fog today—not so heavy after all—having dissipated. I had no idea how to corroborate Buddy's claims, and I was wary about putting a ton of time into something that might not pan out. I would proceed with caution.

Chapter Six
Local Heroes

Theft Deemed a Snake-Napping

The recent theft of twelve snakes and two adult iguanas from The Land of Reptiles in Stockville may be a snake-napping, according to county police, who say they are puzzled by the "ransom note" discovered under one of the empty cages.

"Big Bill's looking for you," Milton said when I entered the newsroom. His desk was right by the door, and I was accustomed to a friendlier greeting. He looked back down at his copy, but in an instant I had detected a familiar expression, one I had seen on Jake's face the few times I was about to "catch it" from my folks, a cocktail of discomfort, slight amusement, and empathy.

Big Bill's door was shut, which was unusual and put me further on guard. I gave a gentle rap.

"Come in. Where ya been?"

"Oh, out and about." What, was he keeping tabs on me now?

"We have a problem," my editor said, handing me an issue from a few weeks earlier. On the bottom right of the front page was my article about John Strauss, a Congressional Medal of Honor Hero, a piece I thought came out great.

"The V.A. called this morning," BB said, tapping on the photo of

Strauss's face. "I got two calls, in fact—they're ver-ry upset. They have no record of this Strauss fellow winning the Medal of Honor. In fact, the Army has no record of him being in the military at all."

And that was the peculiar thing. Earnest as he was—he had shown me his Medal of Honor along with various citations and other medals—I had to confess (to myself) that John Strauss had not looked like a military hero. For starters, he was obese, morbidly so, 350-plus pounds. But he had claimed to serve in the Korean War, long enough ago to give him plenty of time to put on the excess poundage.

In my defense, Strauss *had* looked like a seriously wounded man. He walked with a limp—which he attributed to shrapnel fragments in his leg—and a deep scar stretched across his wide forehead, where he claimed a metal plate had been inserted.

The medals had certainly looked real, but how could I know? The rusted license plate on his beat-up Chrysler New Yorker had a U.S. Marine insignia on it, and the story he told was fantastic: As a sergeant, he had risked his life, exhibiting heroism way beyond the call of duty, to rescue four downed pilots—one of whom, a major, had himself received the Medal of Honor six months earlier for his own extraordinary actions. The benign-looking wife who served us coffee and cake must have known her husband was feeding me a crock of bull. Had she simply been thinking, "Oh well, there John goes again. Harmless enough."

"It's a serious lesson on the importance of checking one's sources, that's all," Big Bill said now, asking me to write a retraction for the forthcoming issue. I had no idea what that entailed: *A humongous mistake was made the other day by a young woman disguised as a newspaper reporter.* Hopefully, Catherine would show me; I hadn't asked her for assistance in at least a week.

"This is basic Journalism 101," Big Bill added.

Well, no one had ever spoken to me about vetting my stories. In fact, my editor had to be feeling a tad guilty because he was the one who had given me Strauss's number after our "hero" called the paper. I had never checked any of my other sources and so far everything else seemed to have been on the up and up. I hadn't asked to see Jim

Bonner's driver's license. Perhaps he was an imposter, too? And for that matter, were those real ducks in the Severna Park pond?

A collection of nautical knots hung on the knotty pine walls of Big Bill's office, and for the first time I noticed that the photos and paintings all depicted ships traversing stormy seas, except for one tranquil scene of a cottage on a river with a rowboat in front and a line from *The Wind in the Willows* engraved on the frame:

> There is nothing—absolutely nothing—half so much worth doing as simply messing about in boats.

Aye, aye, captain, I refrained from saying as I turned to go. Well into his fifties, Big Bill seemed old for his job; hadn't he ever wanted to manage a daily or a glossy magazine? Supposedly, he moored an exquisite, thirty-four-foot wood cruiser at a Chesapeake marina. He was an avid fisherman, and clearly the boating life came first.

I was mortified and thus furious at everyone and everything as I left Big Bill's office and the building. Luckily, I had a luncheon with Lieutenant Haley, the press officer at Fort Peters, to distract me. I had told Big Bill that I was working on a story from the base, so I had better get cracking; I had a bad habit of taking credit for stuff I hadn't yet accomplished. It was hard to shake my feelings of failure, but as Jack Nicklaus once said, "Concentration is a fine antidote to anxiety."

The Army base was like a scene from *Gomer Pyle*. Officers, starched and businesslike, walking in pairs. One of those storied monkey bars over a large muddy pit. Cannons all over the grounds and gunshots ringing out in the distance. Lots of guys with buzz cuts jogging. The only thing missing was whole companies marching along with their sergeants, doing that call and response thing: "Sound off." "One, Two." "Sound off." "Three, Four."

At high noon, I met Lieutenant Haley at the Officers' Mess. He was old, well into his sixties, and smelled like this musty apothecary in Montclair, but he walked rigidly upright and with great purpose, as if to say, "Don't worry about me. I haven't lost a step."

As we ate, he droned on, mostly about the relationship of the base with the town and our paper. He adored Big Bill. After awhile, he was breathless from talking, but whenever I interjected, he clenched his teeth, clearly not listening, just waiting for me to finish.

When we were through, we marched over to his office with the lieutenant whistling "Memories," from *The Way We Were,* all the while. In the outer room, General William Westbrook was waiting for us. A few years before, he had been promoted from one star to three, the first black man to earn that honor. Now he was retiring.

It was amazing how names sometimes informed people's lives. I knew a Mark Advocate who became a lawyer, a vet named Dr. Fish, and a pediatrician named Dr. Smiles, who obviously missed his true calling. Right off the bat, I liked General Westbrook, and in this case, it was the dignity of his name that so suited him. He was in his fifties, tall and trim, with an air of authority and a stern smile. In a James Earl Jones voice, he recounted his experience being a black commander in a white man's army.

"What influences do you think your parents and upbringing had on your becoming a pioneer and climbing so far?" I asked.

"Well, for one thing, my father was always there for me. As you know, that's a problem with many black families. We see the hole that makes in character sometimes with our black soldiers, even when their mothers have tried so hard to be firm and strong. Martin Luther King used to say it was easy for him to envision a loving God because he had such a loving family, and I benefited from a similar experience.

"Like my mother, my father worked hard. Sometimes they held two jobs to provide everything we needed, and more, for my sister and me. I mean, I suppose there was courage and talent latent in our genes just waiting to be harvested," he said. "I don't intend to sound boastful, but as you might know my sister is a famous trailblazer in her own right—Geraldine Westbrook? She's a concert pianist."

"Wow. That's amazing," I said, although I hadn't heard of her. "Is she older or younger than you?"

"Two years younger." Westbrook inched his chair closer to the table and leaned toward me, "But, say, listen, I'd rather you didn't mention her in your article." He sat Army upright again. "It's a privacy thing."

"I understand completely," I said. "So, have you encountered a lot of racism in the military?"

"Why would you ask that?" he snapped.

"I just wondered."

"Well, I will tell you—off the record—yes! But then there's a lot of racism everywhere still. My father, my hero in many ways, could be a racist, too."

We sat quietly for awhile after that until the general continued. "You asked about my upbringing. I think there was something else besides how hard my parents worked, and write this if you wish. The message my mom in particular always gave us was don't be afraid to make mistakes, that it was okay to fail. The crime would be not to try, she said. I guess it made us feel safe." Westbrook sat up even straighter and prouder, and the bright afternoon sun bounced off the array of polished medals on his chest. "And brave."

That sure was different than my upbringing. In my house, mistakes were always met with disapproval, and sometimes fury.

I shook the man's hand, just as I had shaken the hand of John Strauss. Should I ask General Westbrook for proof of his identity?

The general's profile appeared in the next edition, along with my Strauss retraction, which still had me burning. That same day, I received my ten-week evaluation, another shock. Despite my dips in confidence, deep down I was an optimist, convinced I did a very good, if not excellent, job. When I was in high school, I slept with my short stories under my pillow, afraid someone would come through the window and steal them, as silly as that sounded now.

Had I known about a ten-week evaluation, I would have anticipated Big Bill saying he was impressed with me so far. After all, I was smart, and had graduated cum laude with Honors in English. My writing was concise, gaining in style, and possessing a pleasing quirkiness when appropriate. My paragraphs were getting shorter since BB kept riding me about my "treatises." He also edited out all my [sic]'s, even when they were warranted—but I got that.

I viewed my work as a craft, rewriting parts of my articles even after they were published—just for myself—because, after the fact, I always saw ways to improve them, state things better, expand or tighten, improve the lead or conclusion. First copy/last copy was brutal.

Big Bill handed me his written evaluation, saying "keep at it," then left for lunch. His comments were terse: "Progressing satisfactorily. Developing good reportorial skills, but needs to tighten up her writing and show more grit and find more news." From a checklist of fifteen items, I had received "Average" on twelve, including Dependability, Drive, and Job Knowledge; "Above Average" on Personal Appearance and Friendliness; and "Needs Improvement" on Quantity of Work.

The Employee Evaluation Form was a standard document used for all *Record/Courier* employees. In the instructions on the first page, supervisors/editors were cautioned that two mistakes in rating commonly occurred: "A tendency to rate nearly everyone as 'average' on every trait instead of being more critical in judgment," and "A tendency to rate the same individual 'excellent' or 'poor' on every trait based on the overall picture one has of the person being rated."

Evidently, Big Bill hadn't taken these instructions to heart. Still, he had to be somewhat pleased with the job I'd done so far, considering. Besides, I would like to tell him that this was only the end of my ninth week.

Maybe I truly was in over my head. A few of the editors I met on my job-search trip had wondered. In Greensboro, North Carolina, a managing editor had interrogated me. "What makes you think you can suddenly be a reporter just because ya [sic] finished college and had a few fluffy assignments?" In such a depressed place, he'd be lucky to have me, I'd thought, despite my dubious qualifications.

To put it mildly, I was devastated. Unlike General Westbrook, I had not been taught it was okay to fail, or be mediocre. In my book, to get attention you needed to be a superstar.

I looked at my colleagues. I was pretty sure I was smarter than

Tim. His writing exhibited some flair, and he knew all the sports lingo, but that was it.

Catherine's writing was beyond reproach, smooth and impeccably thorough, plus she always had these great quotes, sometimes from the county executive himself, but more often from Mark, her fiancée—most of which I suspected she gathered in the bedroom, an unfair advantage.

The only good to come of all this was that Connor Hannah called me that afternoon.

"Don't sound very chipper," he said.

"Didn't get cheeriest evaluation."

"No? Actually, that's related to why I called. I was just reading your latest. I think you have real potential, but you need some help."

Another mentor! But I could tell over the phone that Connor was smiling supportively as he said, "Have dinner with me tonight?"

Chapter Seven
Old Morality

Attack Thwarted

A 22-year-old Severna Park woman fled from a knife-brandishing attacker last week after she kicked him in the groin and ran home, county police said Tuesday.

I was half an hour late meeting Connor. I didn't want to leave the office before Big Bill, and the restaurant Connor had picked, Blue Moon, was down on the Annapolis waterfront, a twenty-mile drive. Despite the chill in the air, he was waiting for me outside, frowning, his arms crossed tightly against his chest.

"We probably lost our reservation," he said as I ran up from the parking lot, out of breath.

"Oh, I'm so sorry. I was stuck at work."

"I was about to leave. But I appreciate that you were jogging just now."

We spent twenty minutes standing in the vestibule before being seated in a back corner of the small, crowded restaurant. Connor had been telling me about his mother—they were close—and about life growing up near Harrisburg, and he was now in a much better mood. I liked that he'd been pissed at me for being late. At least this guy was honest and direct, a refreshing change from some others I'd known. He wore a green flannel shirt and striped tie. His black hair was much more orderly tonight and, as before, I found myself mesmerized by the beauty marks on his face and neck.

"I know the evaluation is supposed to help me, but he didn't put much into it," I said. "Obviously, I need to up my production, but I'm still finding my way. I refuse to dash out garbage. But you know what? If I'm only average in every respect, then what am I doing here? Maybe I'm wasting my time and should do something else?" I stopped short of disclosing that my only apparent strength, according to Big Bill, was my appearance.

"Hey. Slow down. You're just getting started. You haven't been at it long, and you're a good writer," Connor said. "Bill wasn't trying to discourage you. Partly, that's just him. He's not the effusive type—surely you've noticed?" He took a sip of his bourbon and leaned forward. "I want to tell you something, though, if you can take some constructive criticism. You're not going for the big punch in your pieces. Sometimes you bury the best parts. I can show you examples, but the one that hit me over the head today is what you wrote about that general, Westbrook. His sister is a renowned pianist, you know, and you don't even mention her."

"You've heard of her?"

"Geraldine Westbrook? Hell yes! She's appeared several times with the National Symphony. I saw her in person last year. She's incredible."

"But this was about him, not her. He's a big deal himself and this is an important milestone for him. Besides, he asked me not to mention her."

"He did? Well, that's too bad. It doesn't matter. You're not writing your articles to please others. If it's newsworthy, use it, Nora. Geraldine Westbrook should have been in your lead."

"But he told me about her off the record."

"He said 'off the record'?"

"He asked me not to mention her."

"She's a public figure," Connor said. "Her existence can't be 'off the record.'"

"So should I have said, 'Too bad, I'm writing about her anyway'?"

"If that would make you feel better. You're not obligated to say anything. She's not just any concert pianist, Nora. She's really famous."

I didn't agree. What was so wrong about making an old general happy? Sometimes, I also made people sound a little better, just a little, tweaking their quotes just a wee bit so they were more fluid and grammatically correct. Was this really wrong—to write an even better story? I suspected Connor sometimes doctored quotes too, though he would never admit it. He probably only took liberties with his features, not with news copy.

I was relieved when we moved on. Connor talked about the Naval Academy, which was trying to obstruct development of the harbor. I wanted to listen, but found myself distracted by that little instigator, my inner poet:

I don't want to be a reporter.
Oh no.
I stink.

Now Connor was telling me how much he loved being in a marching band. He'd been doing it for years, traveling to Harrisburg twice a month for practices. He played the cornet. He was in the Army band, stationed in Germany during Vietnam, "a fortuitous gig." He also was married "for a minute" several years ago. He was full of surprises, and I hardly touched my food because I was already thinking I could really like this guy.

While Connor talked, I found myself examining his eyes, one at a time. They were so beautiful, large and grayish blue, but while the right eye emitted trust and a glint of optimism, something about his left pupil—slightly smaller and less centered in the whites than the right one—conveyed a sense of doubt, weariness, a profound sadness hiding just beneath the surface.

In November of last year, exactly one year ago, I had stopped seeing Ari, whom I had gone out with for most of college.

"Nora?"

I smiled at Connor. "You know, when you offered to mentor me, I thought you were going to chide me about John Strauss."

"Who?"

"My so-called Medal of Honor hero."

He laughed.

"He knew so much about that damn Medal of Honor," I said.

"Must enjoy going to the library."

"And no one ever told me to vet things, you know."

"Must have assumed you knew."

"Anyway, I thought newspapers bury retractions. Big Bill put mine right on the front page, with a black border around it for emphasis, like a scarlet letter."

Connor laughed again. "That's because the whole article needed to be retracted." He squeezed my arm. "Whatcha gonna do?"

At my car, he said, "There's stuff you need to learn, but you're on the right track, so don't overthink things."

"Just make sure you get everything right," I said.

He gave me a quick kiss. Several times during the evening, I had thought of telling him about Buddy and the stakes along Route 3, but ultimately decided not to. I could manage this on my own. I had to generate hard news and show Big Bill I had grit. If there was something untoward going on with the State Highway Authority, I would have a lot to write about.

Thanksgiving was in less than a week, so I decided I could coast until then. I'd been working hard. Besides, my Uncle Irwin would be at our holiday dinner, and he would be good to consult about Buddy's theories, since he began his career as a transportation engineer.

The following day, Friday, a very different story commanded my attention. It had been an easy morning at the police station, and I was putting on my coat when a young officer walked into the room saying, "Here's one about a faggot priest trying to make it with Detective Walston."

Sergeant Jack glanced at the report, then slipped it into a folder on his desk like a sleight of hand card trick, while shooting me a "don't ask" look.

"Can I see it?" I asked, walking toward him.

"You don't want this one, girl. I wouldn't touch it with a ten-foot pole."

"Well, let me see it first." He handed it to me. Three men arrested in Hope Park, one the assistant minister of the church three blocks from my house—charged with soliciting for prostitution. Whoa. I asked Jack for a copy of the report, then ran downstairs to talk to the detective in charge of Vice and Narcotics.

Somebody whistled when I walked in. Detective Walston, a husky, older man with dark circles under his eyes, was standing in the back, staring out the window. It was unclear what captivated his attention; the view was of a drab, gray building and a parking lot in need of repaving.

"I can only discuss what's on the report, and tell you that this scene has been going on for months. They would hang a few soda cans in a certain tree as a signal they'd be gathering. Members of the public have complained."

"The minister?"

"He's a young man, and from what I understand, very well liked. He has a wife and two small kids. That's off the record," he said. "Whole thing's a darn shame."

Back at *The Record*, I decided to write it up as a slightly longer item for the police blotter, including the detective's quotes. Four paragraphs. I was required to list the names, but I didn't highlight the minister, willfully burying the lead again.

Three men were arrested on morals charges in Hope Park Thursday afternoon, county police said.

On Monday, I was accosted by Milton as soon as I walked in the newsroom door. "Reverend Ayers from the South Falls Baptist Church just called. He found Thomas Mason hanging from a rafter a few hours ago."

"Oh my God!" I fell into Milton's chair. Today's edition was on his desk and I saw that my "blurb" was now a free-standing piece on the bottom of page one, containing my byline and a slightly altered lead:

> A Baptist minister and two other men were arrested on morals charges in Hope Park Thursday afternoon, county police said. Thomas Mason, 35, assistant minister of the South Falls Baptist Church, was charged with soliciting for prostitution when he allegedly approached an undercover detective, according to police reports.

The other men: names, addresses, ages, professions, description of the park.

> "We've had a surveillance operation there for some time," stated Detective Walston of the Anne Arundel County Police. All were released on their personal recognizance.

"Who changed it?" I asked. "I was trying not to—didn't want to make it such a big deal. And why is my name on it?"

"It's your story, Nora," Milton said. "Hey listen. This Reverend Ayers wants to meet with you. We told him you'd come by this afternoon. He wants you to write another story."

Catherine, Big Bill, and even Tim, collected around me at Milton's desk, a show of support. Tim looked right at me, maybe for the first time since our night out, and gave me a hug. As Captain Bill placed his hand on my shoulder, I felt a large nautical knot form in my stomach. In a corner of the room, a mountain of newspapers hot off the press, containing my sordid account, nearly reached the ceiling.

The detective had told me he had spoken privately with Mason after the bust, that he was very shook up. Now he was dead because of something I reported.

Because Connor hadn't called, I'd spent the weekend with my housemates. The four of us had gone to the Eastern Shore, where there was a flea market and a harvest festival with local treats. I had thought about the minister a few times, picturing him at home with his young family, but mostly I had spent time thinking about Connor, which I felt guilty about now. But I could never have foreseen Thomas Mason doing this.

Time to recapitulate. The things I liked about this job remained the same: meeting all kinds of people, hearing their stories, my words in print, all I was learning, the biweekly paycheck. Still, though I had just found someone great, I wanted to quit the paper and run for the hills. I was trying to stay enthusiastic but already had my doubts about this line of work, and I'd only been at *The Record* for a little more than two months. I needed to stay almost ten more to make the job look credible on my resume. And I had to stop counting.

The South Falls Baptist Church was made of stone. The walls and floors were stone, the windows unembellished glass, the pews and rafters maple. Behind the altar, seven stone steps led to the ministers' studies.

Reverend Donald Ayers told me he had awakened early that morning. He had asked Mason to call him over the weekend, once he'd spoken to his wife, but the call hadn't come. Ayers had raked the last dead leaves from his yard, please forgive the work clothes he was still wearing: an old plaid shirt, rumpled pants, and beat-up shoes. He was around seventy, a widower who bore an uncanny resemblance to the Robert Frost on a first day cover my brother had given me. When he had finished raking, he'd driven to the church and found his young assistant.

"He came to see me after the arrest," Ayers said. "He was distraught. He'd hoped that somehow the arrest could be kept confidential—"

"But—"

"But he knew it wouldn't. I sent him home to tell his wife, Lori. I really believe she would have forgiven him. She's a remarkable woman. But he couldn't face her, I guess. And he didn't come to church on Sunday." Ayers stared at me, his eyes filled with sadness and fatigue. "He was much more of a man than this sordid account, you know. He was a giving, loving human being. I hope you will write that, too. Talk to the congregation. Some are horrified, of course, but most are showing great compassion."

When we stepped outside, I saw something remarkable. The clouds resembled pale-gray cotton balls with gray-blue underscoring, but there were these intense bursts of light here and there, and from the largest, most luminous burst, rays beamed down in all directions, like from a spaceship. Near the light bursts, the clouds were bright white and the patches of sky crystal blue.

Why was it so damn beautiful out?

Ayers pointed out Mason's car, still in the church parking lot. Two stickers graced the rear bumper: "God is great. Let Him into your life," and "If you're not as close to God as you once were, guess who moved."

"I suspect it was his homosexuality, not his infidelity, that prevented Tom from talking to Lori," Ayers speculated. "In the Bible it is forbidden. 'If a man lies with a male as with a woman, they shall be put to death.' Leviticus 20:13."

Then he said something odd: "I keep wondering why they happened to check the park on Thursday." I didn't have the heart to tell him that Mason had visited the park numerous times before. I guess Detective Walston didn't either.

Despite a cold, heavy rain, nearly seventy people attended the funeral service Wednesday morning. Now in a white frock, Reverend Ayers led the congregation in several prayers and asked his congregants to forgive their fellow sinner and cherish the memories of a man they had loved. At the end there was singing, "Old Hundredth":

> We are his fold, He doth us feed,
> And for his sheep, He doth us take.

I filed the obit as soon as it ended. "They really loved him," I told Milton. "This was just some kind of aberration. In all other ways—at least to hear them tell it—he was a saint."

"Easy for these churchgoers to be generous with their

understanding now—he's dead," Milton said. "They're so hypo-critical. He knew what he was doing, no doubt, and right before Thanksgiving. Imagine the outcry if he were alive."

By three o'clock, everyone was gone, but I stayed. Originally, Connor had proposed meeting me for lunch, but then asked if we could grab an early drink in Annapolis instead because he was wait-ing for an important call to finish a piece.

"I'm going north. It's half an hour in the wrong direction for me," I said.

"Come on, one for the road," he said, which sounded good, if not smart.

An hour later, he caressed a bourbon with one hand, and rested his free arm on my shoulder. "Chin up. You didn't do anything wrong."

"I wish I'd never stuck my nose into that police report. Jack tried to warn me, you know." My new drink was red Dubonnet on the rocks with a twist.

"Well, that would have been wrong. This is your job. He was a public figure, the youth advisor at the church. He was *in* the morals business for Christ's sake. What was he doing in a public place anyway?"

"I hate this job."

"His obit was in *The Washington Post* today, you know."

"Yeah, Milton showed me, but they didn't mention the suicide or the arrest—just 'Thomas Mason died unexpectedly Monday morning.'"

"Well, they mentioned both on the radio, and I'm sure it's been on the local news, too. It's not the kind of thing that stays secret."

"All the same, mine was first, and he was probably still alive then. He knew we'd be printing the story right away. Maybe a few more days would have helped him muster his courage. That's what's getting me."

"Pure conjecture."

"His kids are three and five, Connor. His wife said he was acting distracted and distant all weekend. Then, when she woke up Monday morning, he was gone. And guess what else she told me? His first job was as a newspaper reporter."

Connor laughed, but he wasn't smiling. He hugged me for a long minute, kissed the top of my head. When he let go, I finished my drink in a few gulps. "Excuse me. Well, at least one nice thing happened this week. I got a card from General Westbrook, thanking me for the tribute. He loved what I wrote. It's very gratifying. He sent me a box of chocolates."

"You have to return those," Connor said.

"No way. It would hurt his feelings."

"That's the problem—you're too wrapped up in everyone's feelings. You're a good person, but this job demands objectivity. Really, no gifts. Send them back."

"He's retiring. It's not like I'll be dealing with him again."

"How do you know? You're still assigned to the Army base, right?"

"All right, going forward, no more gifts."

"I'm giving you good advice. Send them back."

"I already ate all the milk chocolate ones."

Connor laughed for real.

After a long kiss goodbye, I headed to New Jersey, crossing the U.S. Naval Academy Bridge over the Severn River as the lights came on in the distant hills, filled with picturesque houses. A half hour later, I needed to sing to keep myself awake. Show tunes: "Camelot," "One Hand, One Heart," "Where is Love?" All coming out like dirges. I cracked the window to force a cool breeze on my face.

"Call me as soon as you get back," Connor had said.

I smiled, picturing him, then yawned so wide my jaw hinge locked for a moment and felt like it was ripping as I forced it closed again. I hated that. I tried resting one eye at a time, a strategy recommended by my high-school driver's ed instructor that never worked. As a last resort, I stopped at a service plaza and bought a pack of Enerjets, vile coffee-flavored stimulants.

Crossing the Susquehanna River at Havre de Grace, only a few lights punctuated a surround of darkness. But I sat up straight, calm and steady, my hands at ten and two on the steering wheel, as that same driving instructor had taught. I was going home.

Chapter Eight
Perfectly Normal

Device Hurts Youth

A 14-year-old Gladstone youth was injured Monday after he pulled the string on an explosive device he said he found in his bedroom closet, according to county police.

The house was a mess. It had always seemed immaculate when I returned after months away, cleaner and brighter than anywhere else. But two bags of trash blocked the sink and Tender Vittles were scattered on the floor near Mrs. Lampson's dish. I could hear the television in the den, but my father hadn't heard me come in. He was laughing out loud as he watched the end of M*A*S*H.

"Dad?" Only nine o'clock, but he was already in his yellow pajamas.

"Nor-rah," he said, jumping up from his seat and gesturing to the TV. "I love this show."

I smiled. "I know. Where's Mom?"

"In the bedroom, where else? Hey, it's great to see you." He wrapped me up in his big arms.

He always smelled the same, like the repair shop in the back of his store, to me a pleasant mix of metals, cut wires, and wall-to-wall carpeting just vacuumed and sprayed with Scotchgard. "Jake here?"

"He's taking the Red Eye tonight—lands at six a.m., for Chrissakes."

"Want me to get him?"

"Oh, that's all right. You sleep in. It's your day off."

"Yours, too," I said. "Let me do it. I don't mind. I never sleep now anyhow—occupational hazard."

"That would be wun-derful!" my mom called out, entering stage right. She looked tiny—was this really my mother?—and she too wore pajamas. She was even thinner than when I'd left, especially her face, which was pretty but heavily lined around the eyes and mouth, I noticed for the first time. She checked me out, too, but thankfully didn't comment on my weight, because I was sure I had gained five to ten pounds in Maryland. Plus my skin had broken out in several places in honor of my homecoming.

My folks plied me with leftovers—meatloaf, salad, Rice-a-Roni—as they sat opposite me in the booth in the kitchen. We always sat in the same places. The booth was red mock leather and I reassuringly rubbed the spot on the underside where I'd picked a sizeable hole in the upholstery years before. I was sweating, but cold. I was always nervous when I first came home after a decently long absence, anxious to tell my parents what I had learned—all my insights—while at the same time afraid I wouldn't be able to explain it all. I was too wound up to eat much, yet I was exhausted.

"So how are things on ye olde home front?" I asked.

"Exactly the same," my dad said.

"That's not entirely true, Stan," my mom corrected him. "We went to New York twice this month to see shows. Oh, and I'm organizing a winter reading series for the little kids."

She worked part-time as an aide at the main library in town, had been there for years. "Do you remember Trudy Mintzer?" she asked. "Her son was struck by a car the other day in Montreal. That's where he was going to school. Killed. He was on foot—hit-and-run. Isn't that awful?"

"That's terrible," I said.

"Crazy people out there. I just heard on the news about a nine-month-old boy that was bitten on his face multiple times by a ferret. Some pet. Who keeps a ferret anyway, especially if you have a baby?"

My dad patted her on the head, turning to me. "Nora, you look like you're going to fall asleep in your seat. Why don't you go to bed?"

"I am really tired. I'd love to talk more, but maybe I should sleep first."

Upstairs, the weight of the world descended upon me. Save for a new blanket and two very modern lamps, my bedroom looked exactly the same as when I left for college, as if it had been in deep freeze. The cat had followed me. My mother had named her for her second-grade teacher who had been murdered, gangland-style, a case of mistaken identity.

When I was twelve, my parents had converted the two-car garage into a master bedroom suite, and let me move me into their old room on the second floor, the former master bedroom. Jake didn't mind because he already occupied another large bedroom, down the end of a long hall and very private.

Jake's was the room where the fire had started that killed the young teenager, Karen Braverman, and her parents. The parents had died in my new room; Karen right outside their door. I had always wondered how Jake could live in the dead girl's room, and moving into her parents' bedroom was the bravest thing I had done in my life thus far. But I was comfortable enough there, maybe because I was used to seeing my parents very much alive in that room. One of the walls was mirrored, and I had often watched my father readying for an evening out. He would stand in front of the glass, fixing his tie and singing to my mother while she dressed, usually that Frank Sinatra song, *Lovely, never, never change...*

When I was a teen, I had worked for a charity named for Karen, and one Saturday when we were collecting money outside a department store, a woman with young kids stopped by our table and gave me a check for one hundred dollars.

"My name's Jan Braverman," she said. "Karen was my sister. I was away at college when they had the fire."

What most surprised me was this woman's curly, blonde hair. I had always pictured Karen's hair as jet black, but now that seemed unlikely.

"I'm Nora," I said. "I live in your old house now."

The woman smiled. "We were very happy there," she said, her voice breaking a little. "I hope you are, too."

My mother had given me carte blanche for decorating my new room, and one of the walls was still covered with quotations written in marker on colored construction paper, now greatly faded. Mainly the quotes were about truth or writing: Thoreau, Graham Greene, Hermann Hesse, May Sarton…

And really my dream since I first held a pencil and learned to print had been to write creatively—not articles about fire department rummage sales, dilapidated train stations, special ed classes, or possible state highway malfeasance. But one had to earn a living, and also, as Françoise Sagan reminded me, "I shall write badly if I do not live." In his own words, Connor had said the same thing.

My favorite quote was by Jean-Paul Sartre:

> You know, it's quite a job starting to love somebody.
> You have to have energy, generosity, blindness. There is
> even a moment in the very beginning when you have to
> jump across a precipice: if you think about it you don't
> do it. I know I'll never jump again.

This one was added to the wall later, in college, when I was still going out with Ari, my first true love, even though he had graduated and was acting strange, evasive about getting together. "It's hard when you're in the real world," he said. "You'll see."

I had told Connor all about Ari at the bar that afternoon. "It's taken me awhile to get over it," I said. "We went out for more than two years, and it ended badly—just last Thanksgiving."

When I had come home for the holiday last year, Ari had at last asked me to meet him for brunch in the Village before I went back to school. I arrived to find Scott, his best friend from high school, and Scott's long-time girlfriend Joanne at the table with him.

I remember him picking apart everything I said, and when he excused himself to go to the bathroom, Scott said, "We were so surprised when Ari told us you were coming today."

"Why's that?" I asked.

"Uh, because he's living with Julie now."

It felt like someone had boxed my ears. I felt out of breath, as if I'd flown off a swing and had the wind knocked out of me. Joanne was saying, "Oh my God, we thought you knew. That's horrible, Nora. He should have told you. That's not right. That's really screwed up."

I put on my coat, and when Ari returned, I said, "I'm going."

He looked at Scott and Joanne, knowing they must have told me. I wondered now if they had staged the whole scene, because all Ari said was "You sure?" then started to walk me out, his hand on the back of my shoulder.

"Leave me alone," I hissed, freeing myself.

And that was it. I never heard from him again.

"What a jerk," Connor had said when I finished the story. Already it was evident that he was a much more caring and accepting person. He certainly made me feel better about myself, seeming to appreciate everything Ari took for granted—me specifically. "And what kind of name is Ari anyway?" Connor asked.

Like Ari Ben Canaan in *Exodus* I wanted to say, but didn't. "What do you mean? His name was the best thing about him. What kind of name is Connor? Or Nora for that matter?"

"I love the name 'Nora.' Anyway, he must be crazy, and I can't believe no one else has snatched you," he said, sounding even older than his thirty-four years.

That made me happy. I was lucky to be through with Ari—and Frank, who I started dating six months later. Connor was the anti-Frank-and-Ari. But I was still reluctant to jump across the precipice again.

Jake was sitting on his duffle bag when I arrived at the Continental baggage claim early Thanksgiving morning. It was thirty degrees, so I handed him a ratty gray sweatshirt I had taken from his closet, which he dutifully put on under his old suede jacket.

"At least I remembered not to come home in flip-flops this time," he laughed. His curly hair, like mine, was shoulder length, but his was dirty blond while mine was dark, and instead of growing down, Jake's hair grew out like an Afro, a halo.

"Hey, Nora, I loved that column you wrote about getting lost on all those foggy, county roads."

It had been so much fun to write in first person, to put myself in a story. "That was a metaphor—about finding my way as a reporter."

He laughed again. "Obviously I got that! I mean, it was kind of subtle, but well done."

"Only problem was I forgot my byline. First time I've ever done that, and on a column. So stupid."

"I bet no one noticed. I didn't. It had your photo. Besides, you have a very distinctive style, all that well-placed punctuation."

"Ha ha."

"I'm serious. It was quintessential Plowright, clever and corny at the same time."

"Thanks, but it still irks me that neither editor realized I'd omitted my byline. What are editors for? They missed that it was missing!"

"Hey, we all make mistakes," Jake said.

This actually made me feel better, to think that Milton wasn't perfect either. Since he was the one who laid out the paper, it was really his fault.

"I'm in love," Jake announced as we entered the Garden State Parkway.

"You are?"

"I am. Her name's Christa. She's beautiful. And she's a terrific painter."

"Is she another sexy bartendress?"

"Nah. She lives in the co-op, a few doors down."

"Wow. That's great, Jake."

He lived in a subsidized artist cooperative in Emeryville, outside of San Francisco. He worked three days a week as a graphic designer, and the rest of the time painted cityscapes, each with hundreds of tiny, fully rendered people in them.

"We're not going out yet, technically."

"Why not?"

"I'm taking it slow. It's a work in progress."

There had been several of these slow-developing romances since he'd moved out West. He'd had a girlfriend for awhile in college, but in the last few years nothing had stuck.

"I feel funny saying this, but she might be the one, and I don't want to blow it. I know you would like her. I wish you could meet."

"That's so great, Jake, really," I said, though his news made my heart ache and wonder whether things could really evolve with me and Connor. Between summer camp and high school, I'd had a lot of boyfriends, and then Ari. It was kind of Jake's turn.

A few miles from home, we passed our synagogue. "Did I ever tell you about the time Mom forgot to pick me up from Hebrew school?" I asked.

"No. What?"

"Yeah. I was across the street, at that church she always told us to wait at so she wouldn't have to go through the carpool line, and this one time she never came. It was freezing and a whole hour before she remembered. I could have walked home twice already, but I was worried she would freak out if she came and I wasn't there."

"I never heard that story before."

"Because mom swore me to secrecy. I mean, she felt bad about it—how do you forget to pick up your kid?"

After a pause, Jake said, "Nora, *really*, people aren't perfect."

In the afternoon, my brother took a nap and I helped my mom make sweet potato pies. We needed three of them because our extended family was huge. As we waited for the pies to bake halfway through (we would finish cooking them at Aunt Rita's), my mom braced me and said, "How's your love life?"—the question I'd been waiting for since getting home.

"Kind of interesting." I paused. "I've started seeing someone."

"Oh?"

"Just recently. It's brand new."

"What's his name?"

"Connor."

"Connor what?"

I sighed. "Connor Hannah. He's a reporter and an amazing writer. And he's really nice."

"But?"

"No buts. Too early for buts."

"But?"

"I don't know. We drink a lot when we're together?" I certainly wasn't going to offer that he wasn't Jewish.

My mother clenched her teeth.

"But… that's pretty much true of everyone down there."

I smiled, to make light of my words, but I regretted them as soon as they were out, not having planned on saying that much to my mom. You never knew what she would do with the information.

"Tell me more," she said.

"That's all the news that's fit to print."

"Nora!"

"Really."

I watched as my mother smothered the entire surface of the hot pies with tiny marshmallows, which immediately melted into one.

"Your dad's been impossible lately, so cranky," she said.

"He works too hard."

"Well, that's always been the case, but it's no excuse for being mean to me all the time."

Don't ask me. Don't ask me to intercede.

"Maybe you could talk to him?" my mom said.

"Oh, no, come on. I really don't want to be in the middle."

"He listens to you." She waited me out. "Well, if the opportunity presents itself?"

More than thirty of us assembled at my aunt's for Thanksgiving: cousins, aunts and uncles from both sides, and a few others we had picked up over the years—friends or co-workers who didn't have gatherings of their own to attend. Five hours of eating and catching up. Jake called it the third major Jewish holiday, which made me laugh since, along with two turkeys, there was always a big spiral ham.

It was hard to talk to everybody, but I made a point of seeking out my Uncle Irwin, my mother's brother. He made frequent trips to Aunt Rita's den, sneaking looks at the pro football games, even though Aunt Rita's policy was that no one could watch TV during the gathering. My mom had told me Uncle Irwin had money on the games. From his expression, it looked like one of his teams was losing badly. I waited quietly in the doorway until the commercials.

"Hey, Uncle Irwin. Can I talk to you about something?"

"Shh," he said.

"It's the commercials!"

As I explained about the roads and Buddy's claims, my uncle kept his eyes on the set. "You want my opinion? It does sound like they're getting started. It sounds fishy, like a done deal."

"How can I prove it?"

"You need to dig around. Isn't that your job?"

"That's it?"

"Look, there's often lots of hanky panky with highway adminis-trations, what they say's not always what's real. That's all I can tell ya." On TV, play had resumed. "Don't quote me," Uncle Irwin muttered.

"I won't. You'll be anonymous, don't worry," I said, and he looked up at me briefly before returning his gaze to the screen. I patted his shoul-der, "And please don't you tell anyone about this conversation either."

"Shhhh," he said, dismissing me with his hand. "Who am I gonna tell?"

Friday it poured, and my dad surprised us by saying he had several guys working at the store, so he was staying home. After breakfast, the four of us sat around the living room.

"So, Nora, *nu*?"

I knew he was going to say that. "Well, I'm still employed," I said, then slipped into Pollyanna mode. "I guess the best thing about the job is all the people I meet. They're fascinating, and they invariably want to tell me their whole life story, which I find really interesting, even if I can't use a lot of it."

"You've always found people interesting," my Dad said. He looked so tired.

The truth was I did find most things interesting, and I hoped I'd always be this way. By my parents' brief replies to everything I asked, I sensed this was no longer true for them; there was a flatness to their daily living, like they were half alive.

"That's our Nora," Jake chimed in, never accusing me of brown-nosing, even as my father scowled at him.

"Jake, tell them about your show," I said.

"We've heard," my dad said.

"It's a breakthrough, no?" my mom said, but Jake was mumbling. "It's an honor, a wonderful opportunity."

"Speak up, Jake," my dad said.

Jake stood. "Hopefully something sells. I have to go."

"Right now?" my dad asked. "Where you going?" He seemed genuinely disappointed.

Jake walked right up to my father's chair and said loud and clear, "Yes, right now." He looked at me, "I'm meeting Bobby. Catch you all later." Then he was gone.

Good for you, Jake, I thought, but I also felt sorry for my dad. They had never gotten along, and there were a few times when my father had really crossed the line.

My father is screaming at Jake, his face red and blotchy, blue veins bulging in his neck. He lunges, shoving my brother hard into the foyer wall, so hard that bits of plaster break off.

Somehow Jake stands right up again, dusts himself off. "You're crazy," he says.

"No, Jake," I call out from my hiding spot in the den, but my father has stormed away.

Where had my mother hid when my father had his rages? And what had Jake done to incur my father's wrath? Left another ketchup smear on a cabinet door? Eaten cookies my mom was saving? Dumped wet clothes in his hamper? Broken a vase? Mumbled one time too many? Denied doing all of the above?

"Don't lie to him. It drives him insane," I had warned my brother many times.

But Jake said it was just as bad when he told the truth.

My allegiance was torn, and I was afraid for them both—afraid my father would hurt Jake badly, afraid he would badly hurt himself.

This was the same dad who could be so patient and kind to me, who knew so many things and gave me sound advice. When I was a teenager, we studied psychosomatic illnesses in health class. I was afraid I was going to have a heart attack just because I couldn't stop thinking about it. I would wake up at two in the morning with my heart pounding, and when it got really bad, I would stand outside my parents' door saying, "Dad, Dad," in a voice just above a whisper.

In a minute, he would emerge. He favored light blue pajamas then. He would sit in the kitchen with me, and I would tell him my fears. "That's perfectly normal," he would say when I finished. "I've felt like that, too." He would give me a glass of orange juice, and after that I could always go back to sleep.

All grown up, I still sometimes sat on his lap when I came home, and he hung on my every word. Although he was strict with me too, it was different. I knew he was my champion. When I was young, I thought of my father as Fred Flintstone or Captain Von Trapp. But when he got really mad at Jake, he turned purple, and I thought he might literally explode into a million pieces, like a Loony Tunes character.

While he studied a stack of invoices, my dad played *The Most Happy Fella* at full volume. On his desk was a picture of me at a piano recital when I was about ten.

"Time for a new photo," I said, pointing. I sat in the armchair.

He turned down the music. "What's up?" He rubbed his eye with his left hand, the one missing the fingertip on each of the three middle fingers. He had caught his hand in a slicing machine while working in his cousin's deli as a teenager, but he'd never been self-conscious about it.

"You shouldn't be so hard on Jake, Dad."

"He's floundering, and I'm concerned. Don't get me wrong—I think he's a terrific artist, but he can't make a living at it."

"But he's getting somewhere. Have you ever told him you think he's terrific? Do you feel all right?" He looked pale.

"Perfectly fine."

"And you should also be nicer to mom."

He snickered. "You used to be on my side."

"I'm not taking sides."

"Well, tell her to stop nagging me then."

When I learned Jake was flying back Saturday afternoon, I decided to drop him at the airport and return to Maryland from there. I told my parents I had an article to finish, but really I'd had enough and wanted to get back. Being home made me more anxious than the newspaper, and I was eager to see Connor. I kept envisioning us having sex, the beginning only, undressing each other. I hadn't been to his apartment yet, so I couldn't place us in his bedroom, and we certainly couldn't go to my house, too awkward.

"I'm thinking of changing my name back to Plutz," Jake said as I drove.

"Why on earth would you do that?"

"I don't know. It's a lot more authentic?"

To me, my brother was an anomaly—goofy, but at the same time confident. At the check-in, he said, "If they ever give you a week off at that sweatshop, or if the paper goes on strike or something, come to San Fran. We'd have a blast."

He was wearing a T-shirt again, ready for the warmer climes. He only wore black and gray T-shirts, or if he had to, black or gray sweatshirts, like a uniform.

"I'd love to," I said. "And good luck with Christa. Keep me posted."

Jake gave me a big hug. "Don't overthink things," he said, sounding uncannily like Connor. "Don't be afraid."

"What are you talking about?"

"Everything."

Chapter Nine
Fires, Trains, Roads

Rookie Fireman Rescues Child

After only eight days in the field, a "probie" out of Ladder Company 14 in Ferndale responded to his first fire and pulled an unconscious six-year-old girl from under a bed in an apartment filled with black smoke and tall flames, according to County Battalion Chief Raymond Ford.

Connor and I met at The Steps, his favorite bar, conveniently situated steps from his apartment.

"How was home?" he asked. "Trip down memory lane?"

"Unavoidably. But I'm on a different path now, to extend your metaphor."

He squeezed my arm. "You're so cute," he said.

"How was your Thanksgiving?"

"Same as always, but that's okay. My mom, my sister, her two kids. Everyone else has died or left Mechanicsburg. It's not the most appealing place."

As we got really drunk that night, Connor told me he hadn't gone to college, just taken a few courses here and there, although it was clear he had taught himself a lot because he was really smart. He said his father had actually been a mechanic in Mechanicsburg, but after work rarely came home, playing cards one night, bowling the next.

"He died when I was eight, but I hardly knew him anyhow. I remember all these people at his funeral saying what a great guy he was, how much he'd done for them, and I was thinking 'my dad?' He didn't do much for my mom, that's for sure."

His beautiful eyes looked so sad as he recounted this, and his smile even sadder. "You know, he was so keen on those recreational activities, but later I wondered if he was cheating on her, because when he was home he acted almost obsequious, like she had something on him—although not enough to keep him home, I guess."

He led me into his bedroom, which had a monastic feel. He undressed me with care as I fumbled with his shirt buttons and wrestled with his belt. He stood to undress and dim the light, then sat on the bed and pulled me onto his lap facing him, kissing me and touching me everywhere. I buried my face in his neck, grateful to have found someone so sweet.

In the early morning, I leapt out of bed despite a pounding headache from the previous night's libations. I had to learn to like wine.

"You're shot from guns," Connor said, sounding a bit like my mother. "Where you going and why so early? Is it even six yet?" His face was still smushed into his pillow.

"I'm a lot younger than you," I said, laughing as I dressed. "Besides, police blurbs beckon. And I need to run home first, get changed. Presumably you'll be going to work at some point, too."

He sat up. "So what was it you wanted to tell me about? You kept saying there was something you needed to discuss with me, that I should remind you in the morning."

I tried to look nonchalant. No doubt I'd been worrying about the SHA again; I needed to launch that investigation for real. But I was logy, my breathing shallow, so hung over that it was like I was under water, and I was back to keeping the state-highway biz to myself.

Something great was developing between Connor and me, though. I felt it like a jolt. For one thing, we were really attracted to each other.

I shrugged my shoulders and Connor patted the empty space on the bed. I sat down and he kissed me. "Hey, listen, I love your earnestness, that you're trying so hard at the paper. And I love that you're smart—and so sexy."

I often didn't feel smart as I sat at my desk. It was a juggling act: fires, trains, roads, and the occasional snake. There was a certain rhythm to it all, but I still wasn't producing enough stories. Winter was upon us, and the pace of the news, including official movement on the construction decision for I-97, seemed to have slowed, at least as far as I could see. The last three town meetings to brief communities on the so-called "numerous" highway options were scheduled for January and February, which gave me a little breathing room.

One afternoon, I had a meeting with the mayor of Stockville to press him on repairs for the decrepit train station. I decided to grab lunch out first. A substantial helping of protein might inspire some incisive questions.

Catherine, typing away, gave me a big smile as I walked toward the door, so I moseyed over to her desk. "Any chance you could take a lunch break now?" I asked.

She hesitated. Recently, she had been foregoing lunch for visits to the local Stern's department store where she tried on resort wear—bathing suits and sundresses—instead of eating, to remind herself that she still wanted to lose more weight before her marriage to Mark Dolby in May.

"I don't know," she said. "I'm exhausted. I've been getting up betimes, all the planning for the wedding."

"I really miss having a girlfriend to talk to," I said, even one who used words like "betimes." "We can go to The Galley. Salad bar?"

Catherine grabbed her pocketbook. "I'm so sick of trying on clothes!"

The Galley restaurant was formerly a pancake house, and its floors still had a sticky, syrupy feel to them. But the salad bar was awe-inspiring, otherworldly. I had never been to a something-for-everyone salad bar before this one, which conservatively boasted more than eighty items. And you could return for seconds if you had time.

I tried to see how much I could fit on my plate on the first attempt.

I enjoyed mixing various foods together: chicken salad, seafood salad, tuna salad, banana chips, carob chips, chopped up dates, corn relish, bacon bits—oh, and ham salad, and macaroni and cheese.

Catherine emitted an audible gasp at the sight of my creation. She had shown admirable restraint with her selections, solely lettuce and vegetables. "I don't use salad dressings anymore either," she said, a little holier-than-thou. "That's where all the calories are, you know."

I sat up straight and proud, pointing at my plate. "I've gone light on the dressing myself. You do look a lot thinner."

She shook her head, equally proud. "I'm finally out of plus sizes, as they're called, although I don't know what's such a plus about letting yourself gain thirty-five pounds."

Well, she had a decided advantage over someone like me, at five-foot-nine able to eat and weigh a lot more than I could. I was a lowly five-four, and also smaller boned. She must have really packed it in sometimes.

"Seems like you and Tim have reached a truce," she said.

"He's a nice guy, but I never should have gone out with him."

"Have you seen Connor again?"

"Yeah, things are picking up with us. He's more my type. I really like him. How did you and Mark get together?"

"Mark used to write for *The Courier*."

"I didn't know that. So, does he like working for the county executive?"

"A lot of reporters end up working for politicians since they know how to deal with the press. But if you're asking me, I could never be a spokesperson. It's a lot of pressure getting the right message out, and making sure certain other things don't get out. And Pascarelli can be tricky. Mark can't even tell me some things. There are things he won't even discuss."

"That must be hard."

"You know what, it pays a lot better than newspapers, and—"

"Which isn't saying much," I interjected, then told myself to relax and listen, let her talk.

"That's true," Catherine laughed. She was pretty, especially since dropping several sizes. She had dark, thick eyebrows, *a la* Ali

McGraw, and must have been plucking them this morning because I could see a few tiny black hairs on her cheek. Despite her dark hair, she had green eyes and a face full of freckles.

"What I like about Connor is that he doesn't judge me," I said, then thought about it. "Well, he judges my writing—all the time—but only because he wants to help me, like you."

"I would hate that."

"You don't need it—it's great for me. And basically he accepts me as is. It's really easy with us. But I don't know, I still find myself holding back."

I stopped and looked at Catherine whose eyes had all but glazed over. "Sorry. Yak, yak, yak," I said because I'd been down this road with her before. Her expression was inscrutable, revealing neither support nor disapproval—or any reaction altogether. Most likely, she was thinking about something else. She was a consummate professional, uncomfortable with the personal stuff, even though, ironically, she asked about it. When it came to helping me with my life outside of work, this was how I sized up Catherine: If I were lying in a ditch, she'd pull me out, but short of that...

"Seems like you feel more at home with the job these days," she said after a pause.

"Yeah, I do. I'm definitely starting to get the hang of it. Still not great at digging up news."

"It takes a while."

Mounds of salad to go, and we were out of conversation. And I suppose I was just in the mood to unload—or somehow get closer to her—because the next thing out of my mouth was: "I want to tell you about something, but only if you promise to keep it strictly secret. You can't tell anyone, especially not Mark, although at the right time, it's probably something I'll *have* to discuss with him."

"This sounds exciting!" she said. "I can keep a secret. Promise."

"I think I'm onto something amiss at the State Highway Authority. Even though they haven't finished the public hearings, it seems they've started preparing for construction on one of the proposed routes. This real-estate guy showed me what he insists is proof that the road is being built over a portion of Route 3, and yesterday I checked out the other road that's supposed to be an alternative, and there's nothing going on there at all."

"Who's the real-estate guy?"

"This guy Buddy Gordon. He's a developer."

A strange look crossed her face.

"You know him?" I asked.

"I know he's got a thing about the State Highway Authority. And I'm not sure how reliable or trustworthy he is. He was making a run for the state legislature a few years ago, but suddenly withdrew his nomination."

"How come?"

"I can't quite remember. I'm not sure it ever came out. There were rumors that he had defrauded a business partner, maybe some problems with his company's tax returns? There was definitely dirt below the surface."

"Well, that's interesting, because I can't figure out why he's so motivated about this. According to him, he has land that would profit if they pick Route 3, but he claims he cares more about the community than his own interests. Fishy, right? And he told me he called *The Courier*, but they blew him off."

"Well I'd definitely look into all of that. You have to check out his claims," Catherine said.

"I don't know how to check out anything," I said, sounding whinier than I intended.

"Have you been to the County Clerk's office?"

"No. What's there?"

"You can see if any papers have been filed by the SHA, like preliminary engineering plans. It's unusual to start work before the environmental impact reviews are completed—it might even be illegal, I'm not sure—and the reviews are still underway, right?"

"I think the environmental reviews are done because they've been on display at the hearings, but the hearings themselves won't be finished till sometime in February. So how can you be soliciting people's opinions if you've already decided? *That* sounds illegal."

"It sounds wrong. You can't," Catherine said.

"What would I be looking for at the County Clerk's exactly?" I asked.

"Surveyor's plans, engineering plans. Get the name of the companies who've been hired to do the work. The surveyor's name will be on the plans. You could talk to them."

I must have looked totally blank because she added, "The name of the surveyor is on the corner of the plans. There are topographical plans, aerial photos. See what they have."

"Could the county executive be involved in this?" I asked.

She put down her fork for the first time. "I don't know. Roads are federal, state, and county funded. I don't know what Pascarelli knows. I could ask Mark."

"No, don't talk to Mark yet. Let me make sure there's something to it first. I don't want to advertise that I'm investigating."

"I could ask him off the record."

"No, not yet. Please?"

"Okay. I'll wait."

Driving to the mayor's office, I wondered if it was a mistake confiding in Catherine. More than once Big Bill had told me to be more resourceful, to explore on my own. "Learning from others is well and good," he had said, "but you have to be more enterprising, find out for yourself." I knew he thought I asked too many questions, that I spent too much time seeking his, Milton's, and Catherine's advice. But according to my father "there are no stupid questions," his shorthand for some ancient Chinese saying: "He who asks a question is a fool for five minutes, but he who doesn't ask is a fool for life."

Big Bill wanted me to follow my instincts, go out on a limb, which was why I had refrained from discussing the highway situation with him or Milton—or even Connor. Since we were spending almost every night together now, it was hardest keeping it from Connor, but I wanted to determine on my own whether this story was viable. I just needed Catherine to tell me where to start. So it was good that I'd consulted with her. And for the sake of making conversation, I'd told her all I knew thus far.

* * *

Stockville's Mayor Keating was corpulent, with considerable jowls, and his office was a dark, wood-paneled cave. Throughout the interview, he smoked a cigar that smelled acrid and sweet all at once. This was my second interview with him, a follow-up article on the train station. In the last piece, I had quoted him saying repairs were "imminent." And I had quoted the now-deceased Senator Hogan concurring.

"I've been talking to commuters," I told Keating now. "They feel like they've put up with the poor conditions at the station for years now, with promises every election cycle and in-between, but no results."

"Not for lack of trying," Keating said, taking an impressively long puff. "We're always being told it's in the works, but in the end it don't get funded. There's only so much we can do. The buck don't stop here, kiddo, believe you me, if you know what I mean."

"So who is responsible?"

"The funding has to come from the state. It's the State Railroad Administration that drags their feet, and it don't help that the Town Council puts other priorities ahead of the station."

"Such as?"

"The schools, sewage, other public services."

"So when do you see things finally happening?"

He puffed away, lost in other thoughts, bored with the topic at hand. "As the crow flies. As the crow flies. That's all I can say now."

"Okay, then what do you think about the new freeway that's coming?" I asked offhandedly. "You know, of course, that one of the proposed routes, Route 3, would have a major impact on your town?"

"Oh, it's not going here, no way, missy. It would upset the wetlands too much. Too much protected land, and it could compromise the groundwater, too." His tone was adamant, and he looked incensed. Then, in a surprising move for such a large man, he sprang to his feet, causing the hunting scenes on the walls to shake. "Miss Plowright, I hope you won't take offense, but I'm late for a meeting."

In the car, I fleshed out what Keating had said. Since I took notes in a self-styled shorthand, I needed to annotate them immediately following my interviews or they were incoherent. I had the penmanship of a rowdy schoolboy, and my pages had arrows pointing this way and that, with quotes all over the margins. My methods definitely made my task more arduous, but were all I could manage.

Everything needed to be reported thoroughly and accurately. While conducting an interview, I used a black pen, but I expanded my notes afterwards in blue ink. Fortunately, I had a good ear; I got the quotes right, if altering them slightly for clarity. I made sure to capture the vernacular and singular speaking style of all my characters, as I liked to call them.

I loved these moments in my car. George was like a womb, my shelter, the place I felt most tranquil and composed. I kept a thermos with cold water, snacks, notepads, pens, and even a maroon blanket my mom had crocheted. Being prone to paper cuts, I also kept a box of band-aids in the car, and scissors and scotch tape—to operate on longhand drafts, cutting and pasting the contents before typing them up at the office. Pen marks dotted the blue fabric upholstery on the passenger side.

I would go to the county clerk's office soon, but first I wanted to write up everything I knew and had been told so far about the proposed roads, so I could be clearer about what I was searching for. I liked to work that way, was big on prep, on collecting my thoughts. "I have not yet begun to procrastinate!" as some silly poster said.

In a burst of inspiration, I dashed off a draft of the train station article, then ate an apple. I reclined the seat, spread the blanket over me, and rested my eyes for a few minutes, riding a wave of immense satisfaction. As Dorothy Parker once quipped, "I hate to write, but I love having written."

Chapter Ten

Old Mortality

Snake Owner K.O.'s Thief

The owner of The Land of Reptiles in Stockville slugged a 23-year-old man as they entered a crowded courtroom Wednesday, after the man admitted stealing 12 snakes and two adult iguanas in October.

"What the hell does 'as the crow flies' mean?" Big Bill barked. Too alliterative?

"That's when Mayor Keating says the repairs will be done to the train station, 'as the crow flies.' I think he just made that expression up."

"No, it's something people say, but it doesn't make sense in this context."

"What does it mean?" I asked.

"It means the straightest line between two points, but how does that tell us when they'll get the station fixed? You have to go back and press him. Follow up!"

Follow up. Follow up. It should be his epitaph.

"Okay, sorry," I said, and fortunately I reached Keating's assistant a few minutes later.

"By summer for sure. Print that," he said without even consulting His Honor.

I quickly made the correction and placed the article back in BB's in-box.

Maybe it was the sex and bolstering dinners with Connor, but I had a very productive December. Needing one more piece for the special (i.e., larger) Christmas edition, I phoned Dan Williams, a paramedic I had met at the Stockville Fire Company's annual hoedown. He had offered to let me ride with him.

I met Williams and his shift partner, Warren Cole, at the firehouse. They were in charge of the only volunteer paramedic squad in Anne Arundel County. The first six months were supposed to have been a trial period for their unit, which had nine other volunteers, but although it had been almost eight months since they started their "runs," county officials wouldn't confirm that their funding would continue.

Two good articles would come of this: a sympathetic story about committed volunteers receiving the cold shoulder from the county, and an exciting sidebar describing an action-packed night of their heroic rescues, set to begin any time now. I could put the different response scenes in present tense, a style I'd seen Connor and others employ that I was dying to try out.

As we sat at a table in the firehouse, I wrote down their side of the story, and prayed we wouldn't see anything too gory that night.

Williams and Cole came to the station house at seven every Monday and Wednesday evening after working full time at the National Security Agency, top secret jobs whose descriptions they were unauthorized to divulge. No matter—they were expansive about emergency medical care.

Both men were nice-looking—tall, lean, and muscular—and I really liked their navy-blue outfits. Williams was white and Cole was black, and although Cole had seemed reserved the first time I met him, at the fire station he was in his element. He gave me a tour of the rig, explaining that, just like the career paramedics, all of the volunteers had received hundreds of hours of emergency medical and cardio-resuscitation training. They could start fluids, administer heart-related drugs, defibrillate, and counter-shock. Just the sight of the equipment and stretcher made me feel woozy, but my first article was writing itself.

Cole slammed the doors to the van and said, "Let's take Nora for a ride already." It was nine o'clock, and though the unit had been on "paramedic status" for two hours, we hadn't left the firehouse yet. I squeezed in between the two of them in the front, and this close I noticed that Williams smelled like oranges. It was a pleasant smell that made me hungry. Maybe Cole, too, because as we rode down Route 3, he said, "First stop: The Donut Ditch."

"The Donut Ditch?" I asked. I didn't know it. "Not a great name."

"Why not? Just as good as The Barbeque Pit."

"See what you mean."

The night was cold and damp, and I took in the colorful Christmas lights illuminating businesses, large and small: "Butch's Burger," "Guns and Pawn," "Rex's Big Bowl," "Hair and Now." Mounds of desiccated leaves, not long ago the colors of assorted sourballs, were piled high along the sides of the truck routes, one of which would be converted into a major interstate before long.

Hanukkah had passed without my much noticing this year. Around the third day, I received a sweater and check from my folks, so I mailed off a few gifts to them and Jake, and bought some chocolate coins for tradition's sake. In college, I had lit a menorah in my room, but I hadn't bothered bringing it to Maryland.

Trucks and cars whizzed by as we rolled along, the radio blaring static and the broken-up conversations of other—paid—paramedic units being deployed. "How do the paid paramedics treat you?" I asked.

"Everyone's cordial. We've had no problems assisting them on the scene," Williams said.

No surprise that the Donut Ditch was a hole-in-the-wall, but we got what we came for—black coffees and donuts—and hit the road again. After we had gone a few more miles, Williams pulled into an abandoned lot to park for a while. Toward the rear was a fleet of yellow diggers varying in size, as well as two large cranes on their sides.

"Looks like they're mobilizing for something here," Cole said.

"Could these be for the new interstate?" I asked.

"Beats me," Cole said. "But they're definitely for something."

Our first summons came at eleven: "Man with chest pains," dispatch squawked. "Three-twenty Holland Road, Severna Park." Williams switched on the lights and sirens and we shot through one of those openings in the metal guardrail—those highway U-turns designated for official and emergency vehicles only—to move into the northbound lanes. We were zooming, which underscored how badly Route 3 needed repaving. It was terrifying traveling so fast. Paramedic runs were not for sissies.

"So you have no problem with all the blood and guts?" I asked the guys.

"We want to help. If you can't be a doctor, it's the next best thing," Cole said.

Despite the cold, the door of the house is ajar when we arrive. A 53-year-old man with acute chest pains is on the third floor, clutching his heart and sweating profusely. His sister, visiting from Michigan, says he had been lifting heavy boxes when the pain began and can't stop sweating. He is huge.

The paramedics take the distressed man's vital signs and start an I.V. and oxygen. They ease the man onto a flexible board with fabric sides, allowing him to be cradled in a kind of papoose, which they carefully wedge down the narrow stairs.

Had this taken too long? Could I mention that the man was huge? Did we shut the front door? At Anne Arundel General Hospital, we were greeted by emergency personnel. The man seemed calmer as they took him away on a gurney. He was exactly my father's age.

I was spacing out as we drove down a road with impressive estates set back from it.

"That's the county executive's shack," Cole said. "You know, Pascarelli."

It was a Georgian-style mansion, its façade flooded with light despite the late hour.

"He represents everything that stinks in this county!" Williams said.

"What do you mean?" I asked.

"He means he's a louse," Cole said.

Back inside the stationhouse, the two men sat at a table minding the rig radio while I attempted to doze on a cot, but my mind wandered back to the sight of that vacant lot on Route 3 filled with construction equipment. I recalled my meeting with Mayor Keating, his assertion that construction over Route 3 would compromise the wetlands. How come he was so positive the road would not come through Stockville when Buddy Gordon was certain it would? And why hadn't I pressed Keating to explain?

The only other call came in at three a.m. The dispatcher said a four-year-old had fallen out of bed and broken something, but we arrived to find that a forty-year-old had fallen off her chair and seemed okay, if shaken. We dropped her at the E.R. for a second evaluation, just to be safe.

"It's kind of like that game Telephone," Williams said afterwards. "The calls get really mangled."

I left the paramedics at dawn and drove to Annapolis, the air heavier and foggier as I neared the water. Using the key Connor had given me, I tiptoed into his dark garden apartment. I undressed and climbed into bed beside his warm body. I wasn't sure there had been sufficient "action" to warrant a sidebar; perhaps I should just include a brief description of the heart-patient rescue in the main article about the paramedics' woes?

I massaged Connor's back. His skin was incredibly soft, and he smelled like a warm cinnamon bun.

"Some reporter," he said drowsily after hearing my relief that the night had not produced a scarier adventure. "You should have been dying to see some blood and guts, not praying you wouldn't. Actually, the heart attack can be exciting if you play it right."

I slapped his back. "Actually, in present tense, even the unsteady forty-year-old might seem exciting."

Connor turned over to face me as the room brightened. "By the way, Catherine called before. She said to tell you Mark said Pascarelli knows nothing about that matter you were discussing. Whew, that's a mouthful." He pushed the hair away from my eyes. "What matter, Nora?"

If I weren't so tired, I would call Catherine to tell her how angry I was that she had talked to Mark. But I was so warm and comfortable nestled in Connor's heavy arms. And besides, when I'd told her I would be out all night with the paramedics, Catherine had agreed to cover police beat for me this morning.

"I'll explain after I get a little shut-eye."

Finally I let Connor read what I had so far, but only after he sat through my caveats and disclaimers. "I've written it up like an article, but it's not ready to go yet. The prematurely planted stakes are fairly conclusive evidence—"

"The what?"

"I'll explain them to you in a minute. Basically, building on Route 3 is SHA's choice for that new interstate everybody's been talking about, I-97. They've already decided. There's physical evidence— these stakes they've put along a big portion of that road to denote where the highway's going—and last night I saw where they may be storing road equipment."

"How do you know it's for the road?"

"I don't. I'm just saying it's suspicious. I know I need an admission from someone at SHA—or possibly Pascarelli, but he never talks to me—that preparations for the freeway are already underway. But I'm afraid if I start confronting people, the stakes and machinery will disappear, that there will be a cover-up or something. I haven't confirmed anything. I took some photos, but they're not very good."

"A cover-up? I'm really not getting this."

"Just read it," I said, handing Connor the pages. Then I grabbed them back. "Wait, wait. I can't believe Catherine betrayed my trust like that. I expressly said, 'Don't tell Mark,' and she promised."

He held up his little finger. "Pinky promise?"

"Not funny, Connor. This could blow the whole thing open before I've had a chance to confront anyone. Now they can cover their tracks."

"What tracks? What's this about?"

"There's a highway scandal in the making, Connor—a fix going on!"

"So what makes you think it concerns Pascarelli? He may be a scumbag, but I don't think he's dumb enough to get involved in something like this. In fact, I seriously doubt Mark will even broach this with him since he's knee deep in his own troubles."

"Mark?"

"No, Pascarelli."

"What kind of troubles?"

"Oh, nothing for sure yet, bunch of rumors circulating."

Ah, 1978 in Anne Arundel County, Maryland.

"Well, so much for Catherine as a confidant," I said, giving Connor the highway article again. "Remember, it's a draft."

As he read, I looked over his shoulders. I never tired of reading my own words, but I could see that it was still coming out way too complicated, too technical. There was all this stuff I needed to explain, like Citizens Against the Highway (CATH), a coalition of property owners and businessmen who had been very vocal about their feelings that the new interstate would "forever change the character of the county."

"You buried the lead again," Connor said. "It's in the one, two, three, four, five, sixth paragraph. And is SHA really looking at five possible routes?"

"That's what they say, but you know what? They insist there are five, but really there are only two. SHA says there are five options because they have two plans using Route 3 and two using Route 2, but the two for each route are essentially identical."

"That's only four."

"The fifth choice is to do nothing, but that's clearly not their plan, even though that's what the public favors."

Connor looked totally confused as he read a portion aloud:

Although highway officials have maintained that all five options are fully under consideration, and hearings are still being held to solicit public opinion, a journalist was recently shown highway stakes marking one of the proposed routes along Route 3.

'Routes are not usually staked until hearings are completed and final decisions made,' according to Benjamin Goodfellow, a former transportation engineer.

"Benjamin Goodfellow? What a name," Connor said.

"He's a source. And that's not his real name. He didn't want his identity disclosed."

"Then say that. Say he spoke on condition of anonymity, or that he asked to have his identity withheld. You can't just make up a name for him." He sighed, shaking his head from side to side, over and over.

"Oh, everyone's a critic."

He looked over the piece again.

"So, anyway, what do you think?" I asked.

"So, you're saying these stakes prove the road's already been chosen?"

"According to the former transportation engineer I spoke to—that's what he suspects from what I told him."

"He worked for SHA?"

"No, well, he's an independent expert. He's in another line of work now entirely, and absolutely spoke on condition of anonymity." Uncle Irwin would kill me, even though he had never sounded so fluent.

"Did you ask him why there are five alternatives?"

"I'm telling you, that's a red herring, Connor, a smoke screen, a way of complicating things to make it look like SHA's doing an in-depth analysis and considering all these different options. It's just a way to overwhelm the public—and reporters."

Connor smiled, pulling me down on the couch next to him. "You don't seem overwhelmed to me."

It was after ten, but neither of us seemed inclined to go to work. I kissed him. "So what do you think?"

"I think you need a source you can identify. I think you need to talk to someone at the SHA."

"I know—I said that before! I mean, the presence of the stakes is much more significant than you think, and maybe the equipment I saw, too. But I know I need an admission from an authority. That was the first thing I said this morning. Jeez, you weren't listening."

"Why are you getting so worked up?"

"I hate when people don't listen." I poked at his chest and he seized my hands. "I have an appointment with the County Clerk's office tomorrow," I said, which was a half-truth since I was definitely going, just hadn't called yet.

"You don't need an appointment. It's a public office. They're public records. You can go any time," Connor said.

"You can?"

"Maybe you're more overwhelmed than originally appeared," he said, unbuttoning my shirt. "You need someone to help you relax. I volunteer!"

And although I was just feeling irked with him, as soon as he started kissing my breasts, I forgot all about that, and stakes and roadways. Sometimes he only had to brush by me or touch my fingers and I got excited. I was topless now, grappling as always with Connor's belt. "I'm still a little annoyed with you," I said.

"Huh? Hmm," he mumbled.

By now, he had removed my pants and underwear. We'd had sex everywhere in his camouflage-toned apartment—on the kitchen floor, in the shower, many times on this sofa. I could remember one of my literature professors saying that true love was really a meeting of the minds. "You learn that's the most important thing," she had said, but I didn't know what she was talking about. For me right now, at this moment of my life, love was *all* about sex and physical attraction.

Afterwards, as we lay intertwined on his couch, Connor pressed me about whether Pascarelli could have any connection to the new highway. He loved any opportunity to give it to the county executive, and for a second I felt like he was horning in on my story.

"Catherine says that roads are partly funded by the county, so I guess he could be involved in this. I will need to investigate thoroughly," I said, sitting up too fast. I gathered my strewn clothing, thinking I loved these blue paisley underwear, panties being the only thing I had enjoyed shopping for recently.

It was odd about Connor and me. I liked him a lot. He was smart, kind, and a terrific reporter. We got along really well, although sometimes we argued about the whole "accuracy in reporting" biz. Another one of my interviewees had called to thank me for getting his words right, his meaning straight.

"Usually, I find you're at the reporter's mercy. Everything gets mangled," the man had said.

So, ironically, even though I had reconstructed that interview a bit, filling in some of his elliptical remarks (and correcting his grammar), I had gotten everything right, straight. I had presented the truth. But when I told Connor about it, he insisted again that praise from my interview subjects was a bad sign.

"But I'm capturing the essence, what people are trying to say, their intent. I really listen, and I get it. I'm not just trying to skewer them in some way, which seems to be the national sport of reporters."

"Your point?" Connor asked.

"Well, just as there is truth in fiction, there can be subjectivity in the presentation of facts, and no one comes clean on that. A lot of journalists take quotes out of context to create their own narrative—"

"Oh, and you're not being subjective by wanting to present such a rosy worldview all the time? You're putting their spin, or what you think is their spin, on everything. You're *supposed* to be skeptical. You're supposed to grill them, and learn what they are not forthright in telling—not just package what they want to convey. That's more like a press release. When people are unhappy, that's when you know you're doing your job."

He had put on a rumpled dress shirt now and beckoned me over to the kitchen counter where he handed me a piece of toast laden with peanut butter. Lately I had become obsessed with this one mole on his temple, an inch above his left eye, his sad, gray-blue ruminative eye. He had a great sense of humor, but was very different than other guys I'd gone out with. Because he played the cornet in a marching band? Or grew up outside of Harrisburg and was never circumcised?

Dressed in yesterday's outfit, I kissed him once more. On the doorstep, I found copies of *The Courier* and *Record*, so I went back inside to see how my train station article had come out. Since it had escaped the knife intact, I showed it to Connor.

"Very nice," he said when he finished. "Except you make Mayor Keating sound like a Shakespearean scholar, and I know the guy—he doesn't talk like that."

And my point once again: Was that so wrong? "Okay, on that note I'm off. If I don't need an appointment, I'm going to the County Clerk's right now."

Chapter Eleven
For the Birds

Hitchhiker Attacked

A hitchhiker lost an ear and was beaten and robbed by two men who picked him up in their car in Shady Side on Friday morning, according to county police.

The County Clerk's office smelled like my old grammar school, a combo of mothballs and turpentine. The front office had two huge desks, the kind uptight school teachers barricade themselves behind, and the two old ladies manning them looked like they'd earned their tenure long ago.

I asked to see all the studies and plans for I-97, and in a back room was given a giant, heavy envelope, resembling an artist's portfolio. It was crammed full with surveys for all of the construction options, as well as environmental impact studies. I stayed, skimming and reading plans and papers (and only once in awhile staring out the window) for nearly three hours, taking lots of notes and writing questions in the margins of my notepad since at least half of what I was reading I didn't understand. My conclusion: The SHA may have begun preparing for building on Route 3, but construction along Route 2 was by far the better choice.

As a slew of good citizens had claimed, converting Route 3 into a super highway would result in the division of many communities.

It would also cause significant displacement (about 230 houses and close to forty businesses would need to be torn down and relocated) and would be more expensive than building over Route 2.

On the other hand, there was ample evidence that the existing Route 3 was in major disrepair and had an unacceptable amount of traffic and accidents, according to SHA findings. Indeed, Walter Strahan, SHA district engineer for the study area, was on record saying that if there were not major improvements to Route 3, "Disaster will strike again and again."

It was good I had the room to myself as I had spread out over both long tables, separating the engineering drawings, surveys, and environmental reviews into three piles: Route 3, Route 2, and "no changes to existing roads" (i.e., doing nothing).

Many citizens had been pushing for doing nothing because they believed that the SHA's claims that a major road was needed were based on traffic growth that would only occur *if* a new highway were put in, not if the roads stayed the same. Buddy Gordon had asserted this, too, although he was pushing hard for construction along Route 2.

In my Route 3 pile, I found a memo from an environmental consulting firm named Richardson and Rockwell. They had been commissioned to study the impact of road development on the wetlands. According to a memo, close to eighty hectares (whatever they were) of wetlands would have to be filled if Route 3 were chosen. But although I sifted through all the papers several times, I could not find the actual report from this firm. Finally, I consulted the two biddies out front.

"If it's done, it should be there," the woman on the right said. She seemed to be in charge, but she was so diminutive that she looked lost in her large wooden chair. "Sometimes the engineers pull things out to look at."

"Yes, and sometimes they misfile them afterwards," the other woman said.

"And sometimes they disappear."

Curious, I thought, like I was in a Nancy Drew mystery. In my private room again, I chose all the studies and surveys I wanted copied, and was told to pick them up a few days later. In the phone booth out front, I looked up Richardson and Rockwell, and upon finding it, ripped the page out of the directory with a dramatic flourish.

I drove to their offices in Bowie, arriving just before closing. "I'm studying environmental protection in college and was wondering if you have any recent studies you could let me see on wetlands conservation, specifically dealing with the impact of projected road construction on area wetlands."

"You're an engineering student, honey?" the receptionist asked.

"I haven't declared my major yet, but I'm very interested in environmental issues," I replied.

She asked me to wait, and marched into Mr. Richardson's office. When she emerged a few minutes later, she said, "We'll see what we can do for you." Then she seemed to grow about two inches taller as she said in a commanding voice reminiscent of the Wizard of Oz, "Come back tomorrow."

Along the road, I stopped at another pay phone to call Jim Bonner, the newly elected state delegate for District 33. Allegedly, his district would experience the most upheaval if the new interstate were built over Route 3.

"If you don't mind having a working dinner, I'd be happy to meet you at Rory's Tavern," Bonner said. I knew he had a wife and little ones at home, which perhaps explained his willingness for an impromptu, peaceful, dinner-time meeting.

Over BLT's and "drinks"—I ordered a Tab, Bonner a ginger ale—he told me that although new to office, he had helped form CATH, the highway watchdog group. "As I told you before, I've proposed putting the road somewhere else altogether," Bonner said.

"And what was the SHA's response?"

"They say it's not viable. We're trying to work with them—we haven't officially opposed anything. The road could be a good thing, if everything's done right. It would be limited access, a true freeway, not a truck route, which could greatly alleviate congestion. But we want to make sure all impacts are carefully examined, that the plusses outweigh the costs—all the costs, not just monetary."

I put down my pen for a moment. "You know, I was out walking some of the proposed road for the Route 3 option, and the engineers have already put their stakes there."

"Really? How can that be? I'm surprised since Walter Strahan has assured me—more than once—that they have nothing definite in mind yet."

"From what I've read, Route 2 is a better option all around," I said. "It's possibly not as direct, but it doesn't disturb communities to the same extent as Route 3. And how about concerns that it would disrupt the wetlands in your district?"

Bonner tilted his head quizzically.

"Mayor Keating told me the Route 3 option would never happen because of the wetlands," I said. "And they would definitely be affected. I saw a memo."

"Well, this is the first I'm hearing about any wetlands impact. I'd certainly like to learn more about that. Truthfully, I thought most of the wetlands were in the southern part of the county. What is it you saw on Route 3 the other day?"

"You know what, I need to find out more myself, but I'll get back to you soon. I promise."

I had a stroke of luck the next day when I returned to Richardson and Rockwell and met Matt Richardson, the boss's son, who looked about my age.

"So you work for your dad? Did you always want to do that?" I asked after the intros.

"Absolutely not, just until I figure out what to do next. Would you mind walking down the street with me while we talk? I need something to eat. I haven't had breakfast yet."

Everyone's favorite eating companion. "Yeah, what to do next—that's how I ended up being a reporter." I told Matt about my week at *The Star Ledger* last spring and about Joe and Frank... granted, the sanitized version.

"I read that series. It was amazing. I'm really impressed you worked with them," Matt said.

"I just tagged along for a week. Really, you read it?"

"I went to school in Princeton."

"Oh, what school in Princeton?" I asked with a straight face, thinking his tortoiseshell glasses gave him away.

Matt ignored me. "Sally told me you were a local engineering student. Are you going at night? Johns Hopkins?"

I had a hunch my face was a deepening shade of red as I answered. "I'm not really in school, only at *The Record*. I graduated last May. I just thought they'd be more likely to give me documents if I said I was a student."

"You lied?" he said, but it was clear he found it funny. "I'm pretty sure that since they're being prepared for a government agency, our work is public information."

Matt was full of information, or at least strong opinions, about the highway project. "Sounds like you don't believe everything's on the up and up," he said. "No doubt it's not. As I'm sure you know, the SHA is all about patronage jobs, so who knows who's accommodating who."

Whom, I thought to myself.

"Whom," Matt corrected himself as if he'd heard me.

"All senators and delegates are corrupt," Matt warned. "And all road decisions are corrupt. Laws are broken all the time."

We took seats at the counter of a luncheonette and Matt ordered a scrambled egg sandwich.

"I need to see the full study that was done regarding the impact to the wetlands," I said.

"I can get you that."

"Are you familiar with it?"

"If Route 3 is chosen, a wetlands mitigation plan has to be put in place. It means that while some wetlands would be lost, others would be preserved, reforestation would have to be done, etc."

"Is that true for Route 2?"

"The wetlands are only a factor on Route 3."

"Will mitigation do enough?"

"Yes and no. Wetlands are important, and trying to minimize impact is good, but it's not just about land preservation. It's about degraded habitats, affected fly zones for birds."

"So it's a bad idea to build over Route 3?"

"The movers and shakers see it as a trade off, I'm sure: lose a few birds, gain a heap in tax revenues."

"Jeez."

At his office, Matt gave me a copy of the wetlands study. "I should get back to work," he said.

"Yeah, me, too." I shook his hand. "Thanks so much for your help."

"My pleasure. Let me know if you need anything else—I'm happy to help the cause." He finally released my hand. "Any chance you're free for dinner tonight?"

"Oh, you know, maybe another time. Right now, my schedule's nuts."

Before going back to work, I drove to Admiral Sewell Park, on the grounds of the Naval Academy. It was serene, no one sitting outside when it was twenty degrees out. Frozen bushes, fallow gardens, icy cold benches, plaques for the fallen, and me. No birds, no squirrels. Quiet and stillness.

My brain was aching. I had a lot of information now, both facts and speculation, *To lead you to an overwhelming question. . ./ Oh, do not ask, 'What is it?'/ Let us go and make our visit.* Huh? What could I do with this information? Who would tell me the truth? I needed admissions if I wanted to assert wrongdoing, but I didn't want to play my cards too early.

If only it were spring. I felt I could think it through better then, and maybe be more confrontational if I wasn't freezing. I wanted to get in bed, or go to Connor's. It was too cold to wage a battle right now, especially since I still wasn't sure how to launch my first campaign.

The holidays stalled everything anyway, with the week between Christmas and New Year's dead altogether. When I called the SHA, I was told that Strahan, the lead engineer for the highway project, was on vacation until the middle of January.

"Can I make an appointment?" I asked.

"What is it you want to know, dear?" his secretary asked.

"Oh, just a few questions about I-97."

"Well, he'll be back on January fifteenth. Call back then."

"Can't I schedule the appointment now?"

"Not until he's back."

Connor went home to his mom's for the holidays, taking a week off. When I said I didn't feel like returning to New Jersey so soon, he said I could hang out in his apartment. I felt a little hurt that he didn't invite me to come along, although I wasn't sure I wanted to go anyhow—and, of course, I hadn't earned any vacation time yet.

His apartment was drab and sparsely furnished. There was a black and white poster of Notre Dame, and a large wooden cross above the toilet, which I thought was an odd choice for it, although admittedly it added a little dignity. I watched movies on his black and white T.V., whittling away at, and eventually demolishing, a large fruitcake an aunt had sent him. Robin and Linda had lots of people stopping by the house and asked me to join them, but I wasn't in the mood for crowds and festivity.

During this dreary period I did seize the opportunity to tell Catherine off at the office.

"I can't believe you told Mark about my highway probe," I said when she walked in one afternoon.

"I didn't tell him anything. I just asked if the road had already been chosen. He said he had no idea what I was talking about. I didn't mention any of your theories, or Buddy Gordon, or anything like that."

"And what'd he say?"

"He doesn't know anything, okay!" she said, brushing me off like I was an annoying little sister.

As if on cue, Buddy phoned me an hour later.

"So, when's the article coming out already? Where have you been? Why are you dragging your feet? What's the hold-up?" he yelled.

"Who is this?" I asked, an attempt at levity.

"I've been waiting to hear from you," Buddy said. "Why haven't you returned my calls? Are you working on the story?"

"Yes, I'm still working on it. These things take time," I said. "Look, I'll give you an update soon. Have to go." It was still the holidays, for God sakes.

Chapter Twelve

Connor Aloysius Hannah

Rape Attempted

A Baltimore man was arrested and charged with kid-napping and attempted rape of a Glen Burnie woman whom he threatened with a wooden dart early Monday morning, county police said.

When they realized my birthday fell on a Saturday, my parents asked if they could come down and take me to dinner.

"It's too long between visits. I have the D.T.'s," my mom joked.

"Can I bring Connor?" I asked.

"Sure, we'd love to meet him. And I did a little research. There's a nice-looking inn ten minutes from your house—we booked a room there. The innkeeper told me they have a gourmet restaurant on the premises, so why don't you and Connor meet us there at seven?" My dad would work a half day at the store.

Connor said he'd get there as close to seven as possible, and I wondered if he wanted to come separately so he'd have a get-away car.

The inn was on a classy stretch of property off of Route 2. It was a restored and expanded Victorian farmhouse with two large dining rooms decorated to evoke colonial times, lots of candles and pewter. I met my parents in the large front hall—they were standing under an arrangement of bayonets—and it was nice to see them.

"Connor should be here any minute," I said.

"Let's wait for him at the table then," my father said.

Once we were seated, my mother handed me a small, wrapped box. "Happy Birthday, Sweetie." Inside was a gold link bracelet with two charms on it: a typewriter and a book. "We're proud of you," the card said.

"I love this, thanks," I said, kissing both of them again.

"Perfect timing," my father said, standing and shaking hands with Connor who had arrived tableside. He had an intense cowlick, but was dressed in a tweed blazer and pressed gray slacks and looked handsome as ever.

While my father engaged Connor in the politics of the day, ranging from the gas crisis to stagflation, my mother told me about all the people she knew who were ill, some quite seriously. A lady who worked with her at the library had just been told that she had both liver and pancreatic cancer.

"The diagnosis was so bad she opted out of any treatment, which makes sense, but I don't know if I could be that brave."

"It sounds awful," I said.

"And the other day, nine teenagers died in a car crash. They were riding in the back of a pick-up truck and the driver was DWI. Like I always say: You never know when the shoe is going to drop."

She did say that a lot, one of the litanies of my childhood. I wasn't allowed to be sad, or angry, or even say that my feelings were hurt. Invariably, my mother would interrupt, growing angry herself: "Oh, get over it. You have nothing to complain about. You're such a lucky girl." Her message—you're being ungrateful—made me feel wretched. But her talk about the shoe dropping filled me with terror: Although I was so lucky, it could all change.

"How about those items in your police blotter?" she continued. "Dad and I worry about you down here—some gruesome things happening."

"Oh, it's just random stuff I wouldn't even know about if I didn't cover the police. No different than New Jersey, as you would know more than anyone." I realized that I now catalogued tragedies too—but for a living. "So, I'm onto a news story that will cause quite a stir, if I can prove it," I said in a low voice, attempting to change the subject.

"What's that?" she asked. "And speak louder. Why are you whispering?"

"Mom! I can't say it too loud."

"Then tell me later. I can't follow."

"This food is delicious," my father said. "It's hard to find restaurants like this anymore, well managed, nice touches." He had really enjoyed the bountiful bread basket and complimentary tray of olives and sweet gherkins, as well as the antiquated food selections: Yankee pot roast, Tom turkey. Though he had suffered through the Depression, and lost some family in Poland during the Holocaust, my father loved anything that smacked of the olden days. And he seemed especially fond of colonial times for some reason, although he wasn't *that* old.

"The whole area is old-fashioned," I said, looking at Connor. "Right?"

"I have no idea what you mean," he said, grinning. "Nora's starting to fit in. She's really getting the hang of things here." He squeezed my arm and I blushed.

"I have an excellent mentor," I said. "Tell them about the Bennett case."

This was a sensational story that had been unfolding the whole time I'd been in the area, about a seventeen-year-old boy who had stabbed to death the three little girls who lived next-door to him. Ultimately, through a plea negotiation, the triple murderer was sent to some local institution for treatment and rehabilitation, and could be released in as little as a year because of a new law the State's Attorney's office had overlooked.

"People are up in arms," Connor said. "Although he was given a life sentence, this particular law gives discretion to the psychiatrists to allow parole at any time he's considered rehabilitated and not a risk to society."

"The poor family of those girls," my mother said. I could tell my folks were impressed with how well-spoken and nice-looking Connor was.

For dessert, my mother and I ordered decaffeinated coffee, my dad cheesecake with cherries, and Connor a glass of port. After he paid the check and we all started to stand, my father put his hand on mine. He looked at my mother and Connor, "Give us a minute, please." I sat back down, straightening in my chair as Connor trailed my mother out.

"Nora, he seems like a nice enough man, but he's a drinker," my father said once we were alone.

"Everyone I know here likes to drink," I said.

"I know, Mom told me you said that. But she also said you expressed concerns about this guy."

With my mom, my words always came back to haunt me, and always twisted in some way.

"He likes a drink or two, but I think he's fine," I said. "You can see how smart and well-mannered he is. Besides, it's not like we're engaged," I added, which almost made me laugh because wasn't that what Tim had said to me when we had our memorable date a few months ago?

"I'm saying be careful. Don't get too involved. It won't end well," my father said, sounding more like my mother.

My parents seemed relieved when we left in separate cars, but what they didn't know was that I followed Connor to his place. I found myself scrutinizing his driving— he drove well, no weaving at all, even on these winding roads, even in the fog—and as I reviewed it in my mind, I was pretty sure he'd only had one glass of wine at dinner. It was possible he'd had a bourbon before joining us because I thought I smelled it on his breath when he first arrived. The port might have been a bit much, but "he's a drinker" was harsh. I had no problem keeping up with him whenever we went out. And my father had drunk at least half of the bottle of wine he'd ordered for the table, so he was in no position to judge.

When Connor asked me later what my father had wanted to discuss with me, I simply said, "Oh, he's always worried I don't have enough money."

* * *

My parents had said they wanted to see my house, so in the morning I left Connor early to get my room ready. I needed to make it look more lived-in since I had spent practically every night at Connor's for the last several weeks. From the start, he had been so happy to have me stay with him, clearing out a drawer in his dresser and a shelf in his bathroom. He was almost always home at night, whereas my housemates, like me, were out all the time. Our house could be a very lonely place, and lately it smelled a little funky.

I also needed to tell everyone not to let on that I didn't sleep there much.

As I entered the split level, Linda nearly knocked me over, saying we had to do something about Jennifer.

"Oh my God, it stinks in here," I said. "What's going on?"

Linda sat on the edge of the sofa, wringing her hands, her face splotchy. "Jennifer lost her job last week," she said. "I think she was fired—she won't talk to us—she's just been holed up in the basement with that poor puppy of hers. She never takes it out. Finally, she left yesterday afternoon and we went down there. Nora, you wouldn't believe it. There were droppings all over the bedroom floor and the poor dog was beside himself, whimpering and cowering in the corner."

I sat next to her.

"She keeps the shades down and it's so dark in there. She had locked the dog in! I had to force the door. Puppy's at the groomer now. She said she would keep him there for a few days. He was unbelievably filthy, and I don't know what to do next. He keeps biting his side. Something's definitely wrong with him. The thing is, I'd be happy to take care of the dog—Robin and I were basically doing that anyway because Jennifer travels so much—but she's going to be furious when she comes back. She's obviously gone off the deep end. I wish I knew how to get in touch with her family. Come see this."

The odors were unbearable in the basement, causing me to gag. In addition to the fecal stains on the carpet of Jennifer's room, the dresser drawers had been emptied and clothes were everywhere. And paper—hundreds of pieces ripped out of magazines and newspapers and cut into shapes, dogs and zoo animals, onto which Jennifer had drawn disturbing expressions.

I covered my nose and mouth with both hands and ran up the stairs, where I opened the front door wide, even though it was freezing outside.

Linda followed me.

"This is bizarre," I said. "Are all the windows open?"

"It's in the teens. We have to live here!"

"Well we have to air the place out."

Robin came downstairs, and I said, "I feel so bad that I wasn't around to help you with this. I had no idea this was going on. You guys should have called me."

"We didn't see it coming. We didn't know what was going on. It's all been in the last few days," Robin said.

"I'm not sure what to do next, how to handle this," Linda said. "I'm really worried about her. Where do you think she is?"

"Who names an adorable little dog 'Puppy' anyhow?" Robin said. "That should have been our first clue she was losing it."

I sat with them a little longer, then explained that my parents were visiting and I'd promised to meet them before they left. "I'll come back afterwards. I'll help you talk to her," I said.

Driving to the inn, I made up a little story to tell my parents, that my housemate's dog had developed diarrhea, so they really wouldn't want to come inside this time around. They would have to settle for a general tour of the area.

When I returned to the house that evening, Linda told me the police had called. "They picked up Jennifer last night, passed out in her car on the shoulder of Governor Ritchie Highway. She's in the hospital. Her parents came by—those poor people. They're taking her home, back to Texas. When they saw her bedroom, they told us to toss everything."

"I'll help you," I said.

"We need to take the furniture out and pull up the carpeting," Linda said. "You and Robin can just give me an extra fifteen dollars a month to cover Jennifer's room going forward. I'll cover the rest."

"You don't have to worry about that now," I said. "And I'll pay more, too. It's not your fault." I felt bad that I hadn't been there for Jennifer, or Puppy, or even for the shoveling of the snow, of which there had been an unusual amount so far this winter.

It was Big Bill who approached me about the highway story. "I hear you're investigating possible corruption at the SHA. What do you have?"

"How do you know?"

"A little birdie told me."

"Named Catherine?" Never in the mood for games, Big Bill ignored me. "I have a lot," I said, "but nothing conclusive yet."

"Well, let me see what you've got so far... A.S.A.P!"

So I typed up everything: Buddy's assertions, Uncle Irwin's opinion, citizens' complaints, Bonner's fruitless request of the SHA, the stakes, the wetlands study, Matt's suspicions.

It was the blackest ever outside when I finished at seven, and I was alone save for Big Bill at the helm in his little galley cabin, waiting for me to finally hand in a hard-core story. What I gave him was five pages long with a list of questions at the end: "Our story thus far: Will a new super highway cut through north county?" He smirked at the title, and asked me to wait while he looked it over.

"This is a very extensive summary," he said once he finished. "But what do we have here that's news, that I can use?"

I handed him the photos I'd taken. "These stakes are planted along Route 3. They show where the new road is to go."

He squinted at them. "Where exactly is this? I can't tell. It could be anywhere."

It was true. Just stakes in the grass.

He gave the photos back. "What did Strahan say about them—the stakes?"

"I haven't spoken to him directly yet."

"Why the hell not? What are you waiting for?"

"Too much at stake? No, seriously, it's not for lack of trying—I've been waiting for him for weeks. I've tried a few times to move up my appointment, but we are definitely meeting next week."

"Good. You need that interview. And you need to find out more about this encroachment on the wetlands. Also, who owns the property along Route 3 that would have direct access to the freeway?"

I had no idea, and it was obvious that I still didn't have a story. Too much goddamn work, as my mother liked to say when dishes piled up and clothes spilled out of hampers. Perhaps registering the anxiety in my face, Big Bill eased up.

"Hey, don't get so easily discouraged. I think you're onto something interesting, but what you have so far is conjecture, not fact. Last time I looked I'm still the editorial writer on this staff. You have to dig, ask your questions, get statements from all the key players."

It felt like he was whacking me over the head with a mallet.

"Nora, in the end your hunches may well be right—follow the money, as they say. Who stands to gain the most from where the road goes? This could be a great experience for you. Give it your best shot."

Whack, whack, whack, like one of those boardwalk games. "But I don't know how to figure it out."

Big Bill nodded and nodded. Meaning?

I turned to go, muttering, "I hate this job."

"One minute, please, young lady. Anything for Monday?"

I sighed and ran over to a folder on my desk that contained a piece I was saving for just this kind of moment about the very passionate local taxidermist. It was "green always," as I liked to call articles that weren't time sensitive, even though it drove Milton crazy since he'd told me repeatedly that the term was "evergreen."

I had admired that taxidermist, an eccentric perfectionist who had learned his craft from a correspondence course. He had sworn his name was Todd Buck. For me, each article was a painting, with colors and depth; in contrast, for months now, Catherine had dashed off a weekly update on the inflamed reactions to teaching sex education in the schools. She must have written forty articles on the subject to date, 806 different ways of saying that some people were really uncomfortable with the subject of sex. Productivity-wise, I couldn't come close to matching her.

"Nice," Big Bill said after scanning my lone contribution and placing it in his in-box. "You write well, but remember: Not everything can be about ducks."

Anything I handed in that wasn't hard news, he called a duck article, harkening back to the time I'd written about those mothers saving the duck pond. It was a running joke that I found neither fair nor funny.

"By the way, if you haven't talked to Strahan, who is your source at SHA?" he asked.

"He's not at SHA, but I can't say."

"The transportation engineer who wants anonymity?"

"I promised I wouldn't tell."

"Good girl," he said, grabbing his coat. "Leaving?"

"I need to make a few more notes first."

When I was sure my editor was gone, I called Connor. "Listen, as far as I can see, putting the highway on Route 3 will result in lots of upheaval—and environmental devastation."

Connor sighed. Tired of my investigation already? "Devastation?" he asked.

"People will be displaced, the wetlands will be disturbed. But it doesn't matter because it seems to be a done deal. So do you think someone's paid someone off? That's Buddy Gordon's claim, but how do I corro—"

"Whoa—Buddy Gordon? What's he got to do with this?"

"I've told you he's involved. He's the one who first put me onto the fact that they've already begun preparing to use Route 3, that someone's pressuring SHA. And he's constantly checking up on me to see what I've found out."

"Nora, you never mentioned Buddy Gordon. He's not a reliable source. He's a scumbag. And he always has a selfish motive. Have you met him? He's a money-grubbing, greedy kike, that's all he is, really."

"I can't believe you just said that," I said, dropping the receiver of my phone. It made a loud clank. I could hear Connor still talking, calling my name, but I hung up.

I hadn't told Connor I was Jewish and he'd never asked, though I thought he had surmised. Had I somehow sensed it might not go over well? It was contrived to just blurt it out, but certainly there had been ample opportunities to mention it during the holidays.

When I stood up, my legs buckled, so I sat back down. I was really starting to like Connor, and I loved staying with him.

I'm an outsider.
I hate the news.
If only going home were an option.

Growing up, I didn't usually offer that I was Jewish, but inevitably it surfaced during the High Holidays because Jake and I stayed home for Rosh Hashanah, and ten days later, for Yom Kippur. There weren't many Jewish kids in our school system and, surely with benign intentions, our teachers explained our absence to the class. But in the second or third grade, when I returned to school, I remember a few of my classmates screaming at us as we boarded the bus: "Jews killed Jesus. You killed Jesus."

Another time, I was walking home from school and saw a dollar bill on the sidewalk. When I stopped to pick it up, a boy from my class jumped out of the bushes where he had been hiding with his friends, and pointed his finger in my face, saying, "See, see: another money-grubbing Jew."

Oddly, these cruel, shameful incidents all involved boys.

I put my head down and cried, tears dripping onto my metal desk.

I turned off the lights, and left by the back door, which led to the parking lot. My body trembled in the frigid night air, and not just from the cold. I felt miserable, my stomach ached, and it seemed like the county's fog had come down from the roof and chimneys to smother me. I stood with my eyes closed, feeling the fog also rise from below as it sometimes did when I was on the road, rising from the asphalt and enveloping me like a gauze tarp, a gray sheath.

I plucked a flyer from the windshield wiper before starting the car.

In the dim light, I now saw that the flyer was merely a blank sheet of paper on which someone had written:

IF YA KNOWED WHAT YUR DEWING YOU STOP

The tears started again. Oh come on! Not this, too!

The penmanship was comically crude, as if someone right-handed had written with his left. My first thought was that Milton was playing a joke on me.

My next was to be afraid.

In a flash, I locked all four car doors and screeched down the driveway. I sped down Main Street, checking my rearview mirror for someone in pursuit. "Please no, please no." I entered Route 3, and as Strahan had asserted at the hearings, there was a ton of traffic on the road even at eight on a weeknight. If I pulled over and screamed, would anyone stop to help? Should I go to the police?

I was shaking even harder, freezing, when I reached South Falls, and my nose was sore from blowing it. Through my eyes, everything was a hazy blur. All I saw were colorful Christmas lights, even though that stupid holiday had been over for weeks already.

At 78 Carroll Drive, I was relieved to find my housemates' cars in the driveway. I parked in my designated spot on the street, and sprinted to the front door like an Olympic medalist. Inside, door locked and double bolted, I peered out at the dark, empty street. The house now reeked of burnt Jiffy Pop.

Chapter Thirteen
The Fearful Me

Body of Young Girl Found

County police have found the body of a 12-year-old Odenton girl who went missing after school two weeks ago. The remains of Destiny Deaver were recovered from a dumpster in a strip mall on Southgate Road near Arnold, county police said.

There was plenty to be afraid of, if you were paying attention. In all these tragic—and sometimes lurid—cases, relatives and friends lauded the victim for being a good person, either someone who never bothered anyone or, even sadder, a model citizen: community volunteer, philanthropist, altar boy, mentor, great mother, promising ice skater, friend to those in need... or a young girl who would never grow up.

"I guess it was her time," the victim's mother, Mrs. Ann Deaver, told reporters. "Destiny's an angel in heaven now. We have an amazing angel looking over us."

If only I had that faith, that orientation. If only I'd been raised by Catholics! The best I could do was try hard to stay clear of dumpsters—and highway embankments. As my mother said, you never knew when the shoe was going to drop, and I rued the day I started reading newspapers.

Upon seeing the threatening note, Linda and Robin urged me to call the police, but I resisted; in the sanctuary of the house and in their supportive company, I again questioned its authenticity. I didn't feel deserving of their kindness and attention since, up till now, I hadn't been solicitous of them at all. But they seemed to give me the benefit of the doubt. I told them I thought I could get through this one night without prompting a police visit since I would be reporting to headquarters at eight a.m. anyway to do the police blotter. I didn't tell them that part of my reticence stemmed from not wanting to find myself in a second police report. Or that, having been privy to an excruciatingly close-up look at county crime day after day, I knew so many scarier things occurred all the time.

Trial Set for Murder Suspect

A trial date has been set for a 32-year-old Navy man accused of shooting a Baltimore man and dumping his body in a wooded section of Stockville last week, according to county police.

The first ten years of my life, my family spent summers at a bungalow colony in the Pocono Mountains. I was petrified of lightning and thunder, which occurred so much more up there and seemed so much louder and closer. Once, a clap of thunder resounded so near and with such force that my mother, lying on her side with her back to the window, was thrown off the couch. My father, who spent weekdays working at his store and weekends in the mountains with us, loved summer storms. He would make me sit with him by one of the large windows, admonishing me when I doubled over, burying my face in my knees, shivering at the streaks of light and loud claps. "Watch with me, Nora. It's incredibly beautiful," he would say.

I was afraid of getting older. I was about eight when I first contemplated my own death. Jake and I were playing the board game "Life," which dealt with the drudge duties and worries of the adult world. I wasn't very good at it. I never really understood the game, but as explained by Jake, it seemed simultaneously tedious and alarming, chock-full of potential tragedy. Of course, there were milestones and celebrations: graduations, marriage, parenthood. But I tended to focus on the obstacles: hospital bills, costs of raising kids, insurance policies, promissory notes, and if you made it to the end, the Day of Reckoning. Afterwards, I felt nervous and overwhelmed: In the future I would not only shoulder all these problems and responsibilities, but also be marching ever closer to oblivion.

The phone rang. Connor. Without any coaching, Linda told him that I didn't want to speak with him right now, but would call him when, and if, I did.

"At least Puppy's a good barker," she said as she went up to bed.

A dark and fitful night. To lose Connor and receive a threat within one hour was too much. I couldn't sleep. Since I stayed in this room so rarely, I hadn't changed the sheets in months. Considering that, they weren't very dirty, but they were wrinkled and bunchy, even a little scratchy. I felt itchy and my legs were restless. I loved sleeping with Connor in his bed, and was still stunned by what he'd said; yet, at the same time, it was like I'd known it was coming. Or that something was coming. I couldn't stay in Maryland forever, and Connor wasn't the love of my life—perhaps I'd always known that. The fact that he hadn't suspected I was Jewish—even after meeting my parents—sort of sealed it. He was in his thirties. Had he never known any Jewish people? Our backgrounds were so different.

I couldn't sleep, really couldn't sleep. And I couldn't wake up my dad in his yellow pajamas, but I knew what he'd say: "Try to relax, Nora. Take deep breaths and relax. Lie quiet and still. Rest and relax. It's almost as good as sleeping." I wasn't so sure.

By the time I was fifteen, I was obsessed with the fear that I would die prematurely, like the two girls I was named for, Noreen and Anna, my mother's twin sisters who had died at seven of scarlet fever. That was when I began to believe I could make myself have a heart attack just by thinking about it. At some point, though, I stopped worrying about my own heart and became obsessed with my dad's.

I was afraid of my father's anger, though he had never laid a hand on me.

The older I got, the more precarious and capricious life seemed. I understood how things (like lightning, or an election celebration) could suddenly strike people down, and I thought, "Why *wouldn't* that be me? It's not always someone else." Already, I had narrowly escaped death from spinal meningitis as an infant. My mom recited the story frequently: "The doctors told us you had a 50 percent chance, but if you made it, you'd be fine. It was a miracle."

Statistically, it seemed unlikely that, like the young twins, I would die young, but sometimes tragedy visited certain families repeatedly. My mother often talked about this, too. She couldn't help it that I was born on the thirteenth, but why had she named me after two dead girls? Not to mention that my initials spelled NAP.

January is the cruellest [sic] *month.* I thought about Connor, and I thought about my dad, and I thought about some idiot out there trying to scare me. If it was Milton, I'd kill him first. If it was Buddy Gordon, it was mighty disturbing. I tried to picture my assailant, to give him a face, but when I squeezed my eyes shut, all I saw was a stranger in black clothing, his face obscured by shadow. Or I saw a face that was a blank, like a drawing on a restaurant placemat for kids to fill in. I lapsed into prayer, that age-old plea: "Oh please, God, don't let anything terrible happen to me." Then I cried some more.

"You look awful," Sergeant Jack said as soon as I entered the press room the next morning.

"I feel awful—thanks."

"Really, what's wrong, girl?"

I removed the crinkled note from my pants pocket and gave it to him.

"Oh boy," he said, oddly smiling before catching himself. "I'm sorry. We do see this kind of thing from time to time, but I've never seen anyone act on them. Most crimes are not announced." He handed the paper back. "You need to report this to Dick Tracy, girl."

"I do?"

Dick Tracy was Detective Walston, whom, of course, I'd met before. In fact, I had recently written a nice feature about him. He used to be in charge of Homicide. "I've seen a man die every way a man can die," he had told me. He had dug up bodies by hand so as not to destroy evidence.

"Worried about this?" he asked after glancing at the note. "Any chance it's a hoax?"

"I've thought of that. I guess it's possible. It does seem like the grammar is purposeful—it's preposterous."

"Why would they do that?"

"To throw me off? Like a red herring?"

Walston smiled. He would look so much better if he fixed the giant chip in his front tooth. "It's an interesting idea," he said. "Are you working on anything sensitive?"

I told him about my investigation, that I'd been putting out feelers all over the place, though unlike him—he had solved over one thousand cases during his career—I was far from drawing any conclusions, from figuring things out.

"Personally, I think someone's just trying to make you take a step back, but let us know if they persist. Oh, and I need you to fill out this report," he said, sliding me the all-familiar police form.

I thanked him, grateful that I got to choose what appeared in the police blotter.

And here was the biggest surprise. Standing outside the police station, staring at the words "Anne Arundel County Police Headquarters" carved into the limestone façade, I realized that, despite my historically cowardly constitution, I didn't feel terribly frightened at the moment. I wouldn't have thought I could push on, but, hey, I'd already done too much work on this story—no way was I going to back off now. Later in life, I might remember this as an incredibly stupid decision, or maybe this decision would result in my not being around later in life.

Such a flair for the dramatic, Nora—my mother's voice in my head. Well, it took one to know one.

I felt more unnerved by Connor's repeated calls to the newspaper office. The first two times I heard his voice, I hung up, but I didn't want to have to explain things to Jeannie, the switchboard operator, so I took his third call.

"Connor, please, at some point we can talk, but I'm not up to it right now."

"It was a stupid thing to say, but—"

"Thank you for that."

"Please meet me—anywhere."

"I can't right now. Give me a little time. I'll call you."

At last I sat down with Walter Strahan, SHA district engineer. His office was in the big state highway facility just off of Route 2. It reminded me of buildings I had temped in one college summer: cold tan bricks, unadorned windows, excessively air-conditioned cubicles. The lunchroom would have unpadded metal chairs and unenticing vending machines.

Strahan's office was large, cold and nondescript. Framed surveys covered the walls. He looked like a political boss, although he had beautiful wavy white hair and very white teeth.

"Miss Plowright," he said, standing up from his desk to greet me at the door as his secretary gracefully retreated. She was good at walking backwards. "What can I do for you?"

"Well, I have some questions about the new freeway."

He literally arched his back. "Cripes, I can hardly believe there can be more questions after all the public forums we've had. I was hoping you might be here to discuss some of our other, very interesting, projects."

"Must be a headache for you, all the dissension—and I understand you're relatively new to Maryland?"

He nodded "yes" and we sat. "Done your research, I see. Yeah, going on one year. But I'm new to Maryland, not the work. I held the same job in Minnesota."

"So what brought you here?" I asked. New approach: butter up the suspect.

"Well, if you really want to know, my wife died, my kids are grown, and I wanted a change of scenery. My brother lives in Virginia and one of my sons in Georgia. That, and crazy as it sounds given how damn cold it's been of late, the winters are supposed to be much milder here."

I laughed. "Yeah, I thought that, too." During the lull, I contemplated the most tactful way to confront him, then decided to continue the small talk. "I guess they wanted someone with a record of trustworthiness after your predecessor's sudden exit."

Strahan bristled. "Yeah, yeah, I read all about that in your papers before I came. Everyone had a field day with that. It was a peculiar sideline for him to pursue."

The former district engineer had stolen signs from area businesses, which he then sold to other businesses. He had been indicted on counts of larceny and bribery.

"Anyway," I said, straightening the open notebook on my lap, "I want to ask you—bottom line—is the Route 3 option a done deal for where the new freeway is going?"

"Well, as I'm sure you know, we are complying with all the requirements. We are thoroughly investigating all five options, and heavily weighing public opinion. It's ongoing. But, having said that, in a way you could be right—that is, construction on Route 3 *appears* to be the best option, if you want me to give you my sense, or bias, based on what we've learned. There's nothing that prevents us from having an opinion as long as we're open-minded, right?"

"But this is a change from your earlier stance." I took out the article Catherine had written after attending one of the first public hearings. "Back in October, you said your administration, quote 'has nothing definite in mind, and that alternatives are constantly being modified to accommodate the public's wishes.'"

"We are still open to meeting with anyone concerned, both to present facts and receive opinions," Strahan said.

"Yes, but you are leaning heavily in one direction—no pun intended," I said, wondering if I could use that somewhere. "What about the communities that will be disrupted, like Stockville? If you use Route 3, so many houses and businesses will have to be leveled—and this is so much less true if you build over Route 2."

"We care about communities. The choice will be made with compassion, consideration, and compensation—we've always said that. But there are other factors."

"Such as?"

"You've been poking around. You tell me."

Huh?

"Look," Strahan went on. "From a traffic flow and feasibility standpoint, Route 3 is a much better choice. Trust me."

"A lot of people disagree. And what about the wetlands? Won't filling them in cause environmental harm?"

"Relatively speaking, there's very little affected wetlands. We're only talking forty hectares or so at most."

I thought I'd read close to eighty hectares. Like an alcoholic giving an accounting, Strahan had cut consumption in half. "Hectares?"

"One hectare equals 2.471 acres."

"That's a lot!"

"I'll say it again: It's all relative."

"Relative to what?"

"Relative to what is gained."

I was putting stars all over my notepad now and couldn't believe how forthcoming this guy was being.

"When Route 100 was being improved, it resulted in a serious wetlands mitigation plan and only about"—I did the math—"thirteen hectares were involved then," I said. "Still, that was a big deal. There was a lot of concern, and it garnered a lot of press."

"Well, progress has been made since then," Strahan said. "And, again, there are a lot of different incentives for picking Route 3. Hey, don't write that, please. You're not planning on printing this, are you?"

"Of course I am," I said. "I'm writing an article. This is an interview." God! I took a deep breath. "Can you explain what you mean about incentives? Because I have to tell you, someone showed me a while ago that Route 3 was already staked even though the public hearings are still underway. Is pressure being brought to bear?"

Strahan, who had been reclining, kicked his metal desk drawer hard, causing me to stand up. "Sit down!" he said. "Listen, we did nothing wrong there. We aren't doing anything wrong, period, and it's ludicrous to suggest that. It's all part of the investigation into feasibility. And—if the tape recorder's running—I want to explain that all I mean about incentives is more decent roads for everyone, improved surfaces, better access to Baltimore and Annapolis, fewer accidents, less noise.

"Christ, uh cripes, we're trying to help people, not to mention that Route 3 seems to be the most economical way to go, better use of tax dollars, etc. Look, I have no idea—and please write this down ver-ba-tim—there is no pressure being brought to bear. Are special interest groups weighing in? Yes, but this is a democracy last time I looked, right to free speech and all that. Okay, that's enough now. I need to wrap this up."

Frantic scribbling, constellations of stars. Was he telling the truth? Did it make any sense? And from my digging so far, it seemed that building on Route 2 would be more economical. DOUBLE CHECK, I wrote in my notepad.

I tried to strike a non-partisan tone. "I understand what you're saying, but then why are the stakes there?"

"I'm not aware of them, but if they're there, that's just good planning." He groaned, adding, "Nothing has been done that can't be undone"—my Shakespearean scholar at last. "There's only one public hearing left, you know, and that's tomorrow evening."

"So, in effect, you're saying the decision has been made?"

Strahan, a monolith of a man, stood, now livid. "Don't put words in my mouth. I promise you—WRITE THIS DOWN VERBATIM—"

"Hey, don't shout at me!"

"I don't want to be misrepresented, is all. Ready? We have NOT made our final decision, but we are pretty confident—or sorely suspect, however you want to put it in your report, I don't care—that it will end up with our choosing Route 3. The stakes are merely good planning. We haven't done anything wrong!"

Methinks the man protests too much. "But you once said you wouldn't ram any road down people's throats."

Strahan didn't answer.

"Can I ask you one more thing?" I said, my voice involuntarily dropping to a whisper. "I was also shown a pile of pipes on the side of Route 3. Someone told me they were for the culverts."

Having sat down again, Strahan commenced brutally cracking his knuckles. "Those might very well be needed to repair a section of existing road." He pushed his intercom button. "Dotty, send Mack over, please."

A moment later, a man who had to have been an NFL linebacker entered the room, saying, "Let's go, hon."

I offered Strahan my sweaty hand.

"You better make sure you've got everything straight before you go to print," he said.

I nodded and followed the bruiser to the front door, a straight line that I did not need a three-hundred-pound escort to find.

I sat in my freezing car thinking I couldn't make this stuff up, and if Strahan wanted to intimidate me, too bad. I was also thinking something really strange was happening, since the more I got shoved around, the more I wanted to hold firm. It was a complete personality reversal. I had always avoided asking the hard questions, making others uncomfortable, getting in people's faces.

Somehow, though weirded out, I also felt unstoppable, invincible, something akin to how my mother described feeling when she was pregnant. She said she felt no harm could come to her, as if she were much stronger than before and would prevail.

Chapter Fourteen

Rich in Beginnings,
Poor in Conclusions
(from *Gates of Prayer*)

Missing Skull

Perhaps practicing the rudiments of grave robbing,
pranksters allegedly made a ghoulish theft at the
Eagle Middle School in Lithicum Tuesday night. A
human skull that had adorned a science room table-
top was discovered missing by school officials, county
police said.

I called Matt Richardson, son of the owner of the firm studying the
wetlands. It was the second time I'd called him since we met, the first
being for ideas about how to approach Walter Strahan, which had
proven quite helpful. Now Matt volunteered to leave work early to
help me sort everything out. While he took the threatening note seriously, to him it was a call to arms, an invitation to an intriguing game.

"Someone's trying to get your attention," he said.

"And get me to stop."

"True, but as a reporter you have a certain immunity, which is so
cool. No one's going to hurt you."

His confidence only somewhat reassured me.

Matt wanted me to drive while he navigated, so I picked him up at Richardson and Rockwell. I had brought copies of environmental impact studies for him to decode. On his own initiative, he had brought some other studies, as well as "road alignments," which he said were based on the road surveys.

"This is getting very technical," I whined. "Does your dad know you're helping me with this?"

"No. Hard to say if he'd mind. Anyway, don't worry—these are like maps. They'll help us explore all of the relevant portions of Routes 2 and 3, and maybe that will give us some insights."

As I had observed before, the potentially impacted housing stock was very different on Route 2 than on Route 3. The latter ran along Stockville, Gladstone, and similar towns comprised of working class houses with tiny lots, check-cashing businesses, and shoddy mini markets—an area I knew quite well, and for which I had developed a fondness.

Route 2 was also heavily trafficked, but off of its service road were gracious edifices: nineteenth-century estates, that inn where my folks had stayed, farms, another inn, and a few developments of "grand" homes. It was strange how close these brand new, ostentatious mansions were to the busy road. A few comparatively modest developments were mixed in as well, like an afterthought.

"That's Pascarelli's place," Matt said, and in the daylight I could see how vast and stately it was, replete with outbuildings and horses.

"I've seen it before, but I didn't realize it was so close to Route 2."

"Wouldn't want a major highway running through here," Matt said.

"Right. So you think this is another reason to put the road on Route 3?"

"Definitely. But good luck proving that. He'll probably be indicted soon, Pascarelli."

"I've heard that too. What for?"

"Inappropriate use of public funds. I've just heard rumors, but he's gotten in trouble before. He's a bad guy."

"He's impossible to interview, I can tell you that."

"Why am I not surprised," Matt said.

He looked kind of cute this afternoon, like he'd stepped out of an L.L. Bean catalogue, with his navy vest and shirttails sticking out. His thick lenses made him look professorial. I thought of Connor and that tight, hard pain in my stomach returned full force.

"You all right?" Matt asked.

"That guy Strahan's a bit of a gangster," I said. "When I mentioned his predecessor going to jail, know what he said? He said it was hardly worth the effort for such a petty haul, that the guy lacked imagination."

"Really? He said that?"

"Just about, and his disappointment was implicit."

"Are you including that?"

"It's not relevant, and to be fair, Strahan didn't think we were on the record at the time. He seemed to think I'd just come to chat him up. I had to remind him it was an interview."

Matt laughed.

With his help, I at last understood the full extent of the environmental impacts on the county if the Route 3 option were implemented. I was now convinced that choosing Route 3 would cause great harm. Also, I was fairly sure that a few of the studies Matt showed me had not been presented at the public hearings, which was suspicious.

When we were done, he suggested heading into Annapolis for dinner, but I begged off. I could tell he was interested in me, and I didn't want to encourage him, although it was sticky because talking this stuff through with him was really helpful. I decided to tell the truth. "You know, I just broke up with someone I was pretty serious about, so I'm not up for dating at the moment. I hope that's okay because I'm really glad I found you."

Matt bit on his lip as we stood there. I was exhausted. I needed to write up the Strahan interview and get it to Big Bill early. My heart had not stopped racing since my meeting with the head highway engineer. I was anxious to break this story before anyone else, although to my knowledge no one else was pursuing it; in fact, only Catherine and Connor knew anything about it. Oh, and of course, Big Bill.

Back at Richardson and Rockwell (R & R, Matt called it), I parked next to Matt's green Celica. "I understand that you don't want to date," he said. "But I'd still love to take you to dinner sometime. We won't call it a date."

I wasn't sure.

"I have a very nice place in mind," Matt said.

"It can be a 'Buddy' date," I said, enjoying the pun.

"Sure, we can talk shop." He touched my hand. "I really think you're onto something here, Nora."

"Yeah—me, too. I have to admit, though, I'm starting to feel nervous." It was nearly dark again.

"Want me to follow you home? I'll just get you there. I won't stay."

"That's so nice. Yes, that would be great."

I called my brother. Other than Linda and Robin, he was the only one I was comfortable talking to about Connor. My friends from home and school worked various jobs in various towns and cities all over the country. None were close by, and we were losing touch. Too much to explain anyhow. I didn't feel they could share this chapter with me.

"So how's it going with Christa?" I asked.

"You know, I have to say, things are great. She's really great."

"You sound great," I said. He sounded different, his voice bright, and I was happy for him.

"It's so easy to be with her—that's a first for me," Jake said.

"So there's nothing you don't like?"

He hesitated. "She's really messy."

I laughed. "Sorry. But it's not like you're Felix Unger or something."

"You asked. And how are things with you? Did you reconcile with Connor yet?"

"No, and I'm not going to."

"You sure? Look, I understand that you're disillusioned, but you seemed to like him so much. You told me he was fantastic."

"I know, I know, in many ways he was, but so what. It doesn't matter now."

"I was thinking you could talk to him, educate him."

"He's plenty smart already, Jake. He's just prejudiced. And it was more than disillusioning, it was a signifier—we're too different. When I think about it now, it was never realistic."

"You still should talk to him. It's not right."

Linda and Robin also understood how upset I was about Connor, but didn't tell me what to do, which I appreciated. "I will eventually. I'm just not ready yet," I said to my brother. "And you know something? It's all just as well because I'm not staying here forever anyway."

"Oh, buck up," Jake said.

I didn't say anything.

"And I want you to think about something, Nora. We don't have to discuss it now, but think about it. There are lots of people who have something awful about them, but are still great in other ways."

"So what are you saying?" I asked.

"Maybe we can love someone who's flawed, someone who's disappointed us, even been mean to us."

I suspected Jake was talking about our father now.

Returning from lunch one afternoon, I spied Connor at the water fountain as I entered *The Record*. Milton poked his head out of the newsroom and gave me a good-luck grimace, like we were in seventh grade. Connor's back was to me, and I watched him drink two full cups before tapping him on the shoulder.

He spun around and his face lit up. "Hey, Nora! I'm so happy to see you!" He looked disheveled, and there were dark circles under his eyes. He'd cut his hair super short.

I had anticipated this conversation, even practiced what to say, but nothing came out as I stood there.

The Record was a one-story building save for storage space in the basement. Connor moved toward the door to the stairwell, motioning for me to follow. Alone in there, he braced my shoulders. "I really miss you," he said. "Why haven't you called me back? I wanted to apologize. I've been waiting and waiting, and I know you got my other messages."

"I'm sorry," I said.

"Why won't you talk to me? Look, I said such a stupid thing and I'm really sorry. It just slipped out. I know it was jerky and horrible, but I love you—even if you *are* Jewish." He forced a laugh.

I made a face.

"I'm serious." His eyes filled up, and then mine. He squeezed my arm, like old times. "It was an idiotic, ignorant thing to say. I don't get out much." He smiled painfully.

"Connor, I'm so sorry because I really like you, but the whole thing made me realize that we're very different."

"I don't see that," he said.

This was so hard. Connor was another man who had tried to mentor me, but unlike the others, he'd sincerely tried to help, not turn me into someone else. He had seemed to accept me for who I was—except, of course, he hadn't known my full story. Now that he did, it was easy to see that it truly didn't matter to him. Still, there was no going back.

"Listen, there's something else," I said, "and this is strictly between us: I'm probably not going to be here too much longer anyway."

I had to stop saying this to people!

"Oh, here she goes again," Connor's look said. "Why were you hiding it from me anyway?" he asked. "I mean about being Jewish. Why didn't you ever bring it up? You never mentioned it, so it would never have occurred to me that it was a possibility."

I shrugged.

"Nora, please?" His eyes narrowed and his expression hardened. "You know what I've been wondering about? This is going to sound horrible, too, but I can't stop thinking about it. What if I had used a different slur? What if I'd said 'wop'? Would you have dropped me then?"

"Forget it, Connor."

He looked away for a long moment, and when he faced me again, that painful smile was back. "How's your story going?"

"It's going. I'm cooking now."

"That's good. I'm glad," he said, and I realized something else looking into those gray-blue eyes. It was the intensity of his stare, that's how you knew he meant what he said. He wanted the best for me no matter what.

He placed his hands on my shoulders, just for a second, then left me by the steps. And just as Ari had watched me walk out of that restaurant in Greenwich Village, I let Connor go.

I waited in the stairwell a little longer before hurrying out of the building. No way would I be able to work this afternoon. I went home and cried about everything.

The next morning, Big Bill pounced on me. "Get in here, please. Where have you been? And how come you haven't been turning in articles? Are you ill?"

I closed his office door behind me, not wanting the others to hear his scolding. "I'm fine. I've just been working on the SHA, on what's shaping up to be a doozie, if you want to know."

"I thought you went on holiday."

"That's not fair."

"You used to be here when I arrived, and after I left."

I used to be a maniac, propelled by nerves and lunacy. I used to come in at five a.m.—in the pitch black—to write and polish my articles, a reasonably attractive young woman framed in the huge window of a one-story building on a deserted street. A young woman all alone. Well, I couldn't afford to put myself in such a vulnerable situation anymore, and this was also a sign of progress: I no longer needed that eleventh hour, imminent deadline as the only way to get motivated.

"What's going on with you?" Big Bill asked.

"I've been out there, doing research, laying the ground work," I said. "I'm trying to get it right. I'll have something this afternoon that you can publish, a revealing interview with Walter Strahan among other things."

I returned to my desk. These days, I slept from ten till at least seven, but still found it hard to get out of bed. I spent more time with Linda and Robin, who were taking care of me, buying extra snacks and telling me to help myself. Because she worked evenings at a restaurant, Robin slept in, but Linda waited to have coffee with me at the kitchen table before she went to work.

I typed for two hours without getting up. Then I took a short coffee break and revised and fine-tuned my article about Strahan and the state of the freeway project. But after he read my piece, all Big Bill said was, "We can't use this. The Strahan stuff, yes, but the rest is just a bunch of speculation. Nothing's documented. It's the kitchen sink."

"I disagree. It proves that the SHA is heedlessly ignoring significant environmental impacts in order to stick with its pre-ordained agenda: to protect and perpetuate the wealthy at the expense of those less fortunate."

He gave the article back to me. "Clean it up. Make it simple. Just the facts, ma'am. All you've got so far is a straightforward interview with the SHA boss."

A single-engine Cessna spiraled out of the foggy sky and crashed in the dense woods. I needed to get closer to see what was really happening.

"And by the way, what are you trying to insinuate about Pascarelli?" Big Bill asked.

"Apparently, he's involved in some kind of scandal himself."

"That has nothing to do with the SHA, and it's none of your business anyhow. Becky Bauer at *The Courier* is following that, and it's merely an investigation at this juncture." He paused, pointing to the pages in my hand. "What's Pascarelli's take on the stakes? If you want to bring up Pascarelli, it has to be relevant to the story you're covering. You need more documentation, more interviews. Newspaper reporting 101."

What happened to that avuncular editor with a son living in Verona, New Jersey, right near my hometown? I gave him a dirty look. "I can't get to Pascarelli. His henchman, Mark Dolby, never returns my calls."

"Maybe there's not a deeper story here after all. Is that what you think?" Big Bill said.

"Then why would someone threaten me? Even though I know nobody here gives that much credence."

Big Bill looked offended, and possibly shocked by my impudence. I stepped back; it almost felt like he might slap me for being fresh.

In truth, I was still not positive Milton hadn't penned that threatening note. He had looked self-conscious, restless, when I'd shown it to everyone. Yet, more than Big Bill, he had seemed concerned. The newsroom staff had huddled around me to lend support, the third time in my short stint at *The Record*. The first had been when it came to light that my Medal of Honor "hero" was a fraud; the second was when Thomas Mason hung himself.

"I can't say I'm not disappointed," Big Bill said after awhile. "Because, personally, I *am* convinced there's wrongdoing, and that it's backed by special interests. I thought we discussed this at the outset, many moons ago. Follow the special interests, I told you. It has to do with the land. That's what I said."

Not that many moons ago, I wanted to say. But hearing Big Bill's words made me sick because wasn't that what Buddy Gordon had suggested at the very outset, too, when this whole thing started? Because I didn't know how to get at it, I had grasped at the details at hand—that the SHA preferred Route 3 for its own reasons, mainly that the communities that would be uprooted had less clout. I'd reported everything I'd gleaned instead of pushing deeper and getting to the bottom of it all so that I could tell a clear, honest story. It was like the first English paper I wrote in college. I had thought it was great, but I received an "F" and a two-word comment, "See me." When I'd gone to the professor, he said, "There's a lot here, but why do I have to organize your thoughts and figure out your meaning?"

It all fed into a fundamental insecurity I had, that I was smart and capable, but not the deepest thinker. I did well enough because of effort and a knack for description, but sometimes I missed the big picture.

Even Matt seemed to have a better handle on the underlying story. As we'd traveled along Route 3, he had pointed out large tracts of undeveloped land, including several hectares in Severna Park where construction was underway. I stopped the car so we could examine the sign, which depicted a village of townhouses, stores, and office space. "Coming Soon: Severna Park's Newest Jewel." This was the project Buddy had alluded to, and that *was* many moons ago.

"It's not just that the poor people's houses are expendable," Matt had said. "Whatever they build here will be a goldmine for its developer because of the easy-access freeway. Who owns this? What are the plans for this land?"

I had traveled down the wrong highway, somewhere veering off the road, lost in my conviction that the hearings were bogus since the SHA had already made up its mind and didn't care that many disadvantaged people—and likely tons of birds—would suffer! To me, that was the gist of it, but it was really something more. Something larger and possibly scarier.

Fighting tears, I couldn't bring myself to lift my head and look at Big Bill, my eyes transfixed on the soiled beige carpeting.

"Come on, lighten up," my editor said eventually. "I need you to drop everything and scoot over to the governor's mansion. They're having a birthday dinner for the two oldest women in Anne Arundel County."

I looked up at him, laughing through the mist. "Scoot?"

Chapter Fifteen
Whining and Dining

Young at Heart

Four hundred and fifty senior citizens packed the governor's mansion Thursday, examining everything that wasn't nailed down: Fabergé eggs, a Thomas Eakins portrait, an extensive liquor closet, and zebra-striped pajamas belonging to the state's highest elected official.

Back at the county clerk's office, I looked up the property records for the giant development along Route 3 in Severna Park, but the deed merely said "Severna Park Village Corporation," with no individuals or development company listed.

And Buddy Gordon didn't seem in the mood to play when I phoned him. "I have my guess, but you're the reporter," he said. "That's what you're supposed to find out."

The all-knowing Matt was much more helpful. "That's what developers do," he explained. "They register each of their properties as a different entity, so if they have a problem with one, their creditors can't go after the others."

"If you say so," I said. "So what am I supposed to do now?"

"I believe they're required to file a Certificate of Incorporation each time with the Maryland Secretary of State. That might give us some names. They're right in Annapolis, and those are public records, too." It took a week for that office to respond to my requests, not only for information about the Severna Park development, but for records of all the proposed projects along Route 3 that could profit from the new road. I learned that a company named Duffy Development owned a lot of this real estate, including the Severna Park Village Corp. A few tracts of undeveloped land belonged to Buddy Gordon, and a few to other companies, but the bulk of it was owned by one Sean Duffy. Predictably, Duffy's secretary told me he was really busy, but she'd get back to me. She promised her boss would fit me in by the end of February.

I followed Mark Dolby home from Pascarelli's office one night, watched him park, and hid my car a block away. He lived in a nice townhouse not far from the harbor.

"What are you doing here?" he asked as I walked up his driveway. His hands were loaded up with used Styrofoam cups and fast-food wrappers.

"Oh, hi Mark. I was in the neighborhood and had a few questions for you."

"What about?"

"Oh, I just wanted to get your boss's opinion of I-97, whether he's involved in any way with where the road will go."

"I can't believe you're at my house. When I'm not at the office, I'm off duty."

"But for me you're permanently off duty!"

"Nora, get out of here. Pascarelli's not involved with the road decision, and it's a bad time. Sorry, but I'm asking you please."

Two days later, *The Courier* reported that Pascarelli was under investigation for using public employees to "build another addition" to his estate, as Connor put it in his front-page article. Catherine told us Mark was besieged.

I rarely saw Catherine these days as she continued to interview parents and school administrators about the endlessly controversial sex-ed curriculum. She had now written a gazillion articles about this, as well as a column exposing a man who had exposed himself outside her kitchen window. When I'd asked if there could be a connection, if he had knowingly chosen to flash the sex-ed reporter, she said that was preposterous, but it sounded plausible to me.

Matt picked me up for our "special" date in a sports jacket, and I was glad I had borrowed a pretty navy dress from Linda.

"Our 'Buddy' date," I reminded him. I enjoyed his company, but remained determined not to lead him on. "What's so special anyway?" I asked. It had been exactly 160 days since my arrival in Anne Arundel County, but he had no way of knowing that.

"I'm taking you to the best restaurant for fifty miles around. It's where people in the know go to eat."

"You're such a snob!"

"Me, right. By the way, you look great."

We traveled forty-five minutes to the Eastern Shore, a quiet drive on dark back roads.

"I had such a frustrating experience yesterday," I said. "Someone suggested we do a human interest piece about this Stockville guy who just died, this friendly old man who hung out at the strip mall and helped everyone, gave advice. So I interviewed all these people and was getting really colorful quotes—I was all set to go—but then the manager of the chocolate shop told me he was a child molester."

"He said that?"

"In so many words. He said he didn't want to malign the old man, but that one of his customers claimed he'd rubbed up against her little boy, so he had to ban him from the store."

"So how do you handle that?"

"You don't. You say, 'so much for that' and find something else. But it was a good reminder to go to the scene whenever possible and make sure you get the whole story."

As we neared the Chesapeake, I smelled that compost of scents I always loved at the Jersey shore, the smell of the beach, waves, marshes, crustaceans dead and living, seagulls and herons all combined. Funny that it even smelled this way in the winter.

"I'm so glad you found your way to R & R," Matt said as he pulled into the parking lot.

This restaurant had once been a mill, and was decorated with abundant strands of warm, white lights. Inside, there were several intimate dining rooms with maybe five or six tables in each. We were seated in a charming room with print wallpaper, flowery tablecloths, and a geometric rug. "I feel like I'm hallucinating," I said to Matt, who was ordering champagne. "What are we celebrating, by the way?" I asked again, although I wasn't complaining. I loved champagne.

"Our first real date," Matt said.

"But not a date-date, remember?" Way to beat a dead horse.

"Right. Fine. We can toast Buddy. Want to share everything? May I order?" he asked.

"Be my guest."

"We'll have the escargot and special paté, and after we eat those we'll order our main courses," he told the waiter. "I don't want to be rushed," he explained to me.

"I can't wait to taste the 'lavish' crackers," I said.

"That's an oxymoron," Matt said, then leaned forward, suddenly serious. "So, I have to tell you something before we get going on something else. I have several applications into law schools, and I'll be hearing back pretty soon."

"Oh really? Where did you apply?"

"Yale, Columbia, and a few in the Midwest."

"Wow, good for you. It's perfect for you," I said. I could see myself in his shiny lenses.

"The thing is, I'm not entirely sure it's what I want to do. And now that I've met you, I really don't know."

I took a swig of champagne. "Matt, seriously, please don't figure me in your plans. Like I've always said, I just want to be friends, and also"—I couldn't help myself these days—"I don't know how much longer I can tough it out down here."

"It's kind of redneck, I know, but there are worse places," he said. "You'd be crazy to go. You're doing so well. You've only been here a short while and you're closing in on a big story. You should feel really good."

I had no answer to that. "By the way, I'm Jewish," I said.

"Good for you. Why are you telling me this?"

"I don't know, in case it matters."

"You're so weird."

"You would be a great lawyer," I said, but Matt was staring at something behind me.

"Whoa," he whispered, leaning in even farther.

"Whoa what?"

He stood. "Hold on. Be right back."

He had a peculiar expression when he returned, sat, pulled his chair in tight to the table and said softly, "Don't look now, but that man in back of you, sitting next to Walter Strahan, is the—"

"Walt—"

Matt seized my wrist to stop my words. "Shhh."

I started to turn my head.

"No, don't look," he whispered. "Come with me."

Like a little duckling, I followed him out, my head bowed as we walked down a dark, flowery hallway and into the men's room. Fortunately, it was a bathroom for one, which Matt locked behind us.

"Walter Strahan's here? That's bizarre!"

"He's sitting right in back of you. And guess who he's with? Sean Duffy, the guy who owns Duffy Development. Not only does he own almost all the open land along Route 3, but I found out something else about him I was going to tell you tonight. Buddy Gordon got nailed for tax evasion several years ago, and the scuttlebutt was that Duffy reported him. They hate each other."

"How do you know all this?"

"I've been digging around about Gordon."

"You're amazing." I was dazed and a little drunk by now since I'd barely eaten all day and still hadn't had any food.

"Nora, Duffy's your man. He's having dinner with Strahan."

"I know he's my man. I have an appointment to meet with him next week, and I was supposed to meet him before that. Are you sure Strahan's here? I didn't see him."

"Take my word. There are four men in suits at the table behind you. I noticed Strahan first. I thought the other guy might be Duffy, and the maitre d' just confirmed it. He's wearing a very expensive gray suit. Anyway, why would they be together? They *must* be doing a deal. They're in cahoots. Your story, Nora—this is it!"

It was making me nauseous, and claustrophobic. The toilet seat lid was up, the rim of the bowl blotted with urine. There was also a urinal with a bright yellow pool of urine in the drain. "I feel really strange in here," I said. "Men's rooms are gross." Of course, you could say the same for women's rooms, which always baffled me because of how few people flushed. Presumably, they did better in their own homes.

Matt shook me. "Earth to Nora. Listen, we have to go back in, but you should talk to Strahan some more, confront him about this."

I was stricken. "Here?"

"No, not tonight."

As we left the men's room, an old man waiting outside wagged his finger at me. "That's not right, young lady!" he said.

"It's gross in there," I said back.

We slunk back to our dining room, my head bowed again after a quick glance to confirm that it was indeed Walter Strahan sitting there, immersed in conversation. I couldn't take in the others. I sat down with my back to the highway engineer once more. Our appetizers had been served. The escargot was cold.

I sat still, not wanting to attract attention. I tried to eavesdrop on the conversation behind me, but it was impossible. I was having difficulty swallowing, then knocked over my champagne flute. I didn't jump or even stir, though it was spilling onto my lap, through the napkin onto Linda's dress. Matt donated his napkin to the cause and two others he retrieved from an empty table, and at last the dripping stopped.

"So calm," he said.

"I'm famous for that."

"They're getting ready to leave," Matt whispered, winking at me.

"Who paid the check?"

"I missed that," he said. "I was fetching napkins."

I felt the four men rise as one from their table, and stole a quick glance. They all seemed massive. As they neared us, Strahan halted. He was standing right beside me, clearing his throat, so I had to look up.

"Oh, hi Mr. Strahan," I said.

"Ms. Plowright."

Then, to Matt's astonishment, I stood up in my wet dress and approached the man standing behind Strahan, who was less imposing after all, more normal-sized than the others and wearing a beautiful charcoal-gray suit and royal blue shirt. "Good evening, Mr. Duffy," I said, offering my hand. "I'm looking forward to meeting with you."

He looked at me blankly.

Strahan kept avoiding my calls. "He's too busy. He can't take a meeting," his secretary said.

"I only need to speak with him for a few minutes. It doesn't have to be in person."

Finally, she said Strahan would phone me at the paper in the afternoon. "But it will have to be quick."

So I waited and waited, and thought about how I hated waiting. I didn't like to stay put, liked to come and go as I pleased. In this way, working at a paper was a good choice for me since I was always on the move.

Testing my patience, Strahan called at ten to five. As before, I had arranged my questions in order of increasing intensity.

"So, just checking in. Has the decision been made about where I-97 will go?" I asked, a kind of softball since I knew he'd have a pat answer.

"Nope, but we're getting close, and you'll be one of the first to know. Haven't we gone over this?"

"When we met, I mentioned to you that some stakes were already planted along Route 3. And at first there were a few culvert pipes, but recently I saw a *lot* of them there. There are stockpiles now, huge concrete pipes piled along the roadside for maybe a quarter mile. This is the drainage system for the new road, no?"

"What did you see exactly?" Strahan asked.

"These big white pipes, huge tubes. They seem to be multiplying. And there are cranes and these Cat tractors and diggers."

"I'll have to check it out, but it could very well be that the supplier put them there because he was running out of storage in his yard and he knows it's *likely*—not definite, mind you, but likely—that Route 3 will be chosen."

"Would you say 98 percent likely?"

"Can't say that yet."

"Well, I'm still confused because it seems like the environmental ramifications if Route 3 is selected are much worse than they are for Route 2, and I also don't think the public has been properly furnished with all the facts about this."

"Excuse me, Miss Plowright, but you've got your facts wrong. The impact studies have been available at every hearing. And anyone can look at any of our plans or other documents. They're all available at the Annapolis Public Library. Your naiveté has caused you solely to focus on the problems with building over Route 3. Did you know that there's a potter's field along Route 2 which would have to be disinterred if the road went there? That's a very messy business which also has to be taken into consideration."

"A what?"

"A potter's field. Lots of graves."

"First I'm hearing about this." Had Matt only shown me the Route 3 environmental impact studies? I had assumed they were the only ones. "I'll check that out, but back to Route 3. Will new development include moderate- and low-income housing since much of this will be lost?"

"People will be relocated and adequately compensated," Strahan said. "Okay, time's up."

"Wait, please, I have two more questions. I'll be quick. Is the developer Sean Duffy involved in the decision for the road? Is he putting pressure on SHA?"

One banana, two banana, three banana, four. I counted seven bananas before Strahan replied.

"Miss Plowright, it's no secret that Mr. Duffy has plans for two large developments along Route 3. He is following our deliberations with great interest."

"Isn't he the person who stands to be the single, largest beneficiary if Route 3 is chosen?"

"That may or may not be true. I honestly don't know."

"Well, based on the fact that he has big plans for at least two vast tracts of land along Route 3, how could you have dinner with him and let him pick up the tab?" I bluffed.

"One dinner is not going to influence my opinion on this," Strahan said.

Bingo!

"He's not bribing us, if that's what you're insinuating." His voice had gotten so loud by the end of that sentence that I was forced to hold the receiver away from my ear. "My God, he's a great friend of mine is all," he added.

"But you would agree that it doesn't look good for you to be socializing with someone who stands to gain so much. Don't you think that under the circumstances, since you're friends, you should recuse yourself from making a decision on the project?"

I had gotten the word "recuse" from Matt. He had written out these last questions for me. He had worked at his uncle's law firm during a few college summers, and sat in on some depositions. We had practiced my line of questioning with Matt playing Strahan. His mock answers had been right on target.

Walter Strahan was silent and I wondered if he had hung up.

"Friends can take each other out to dinner," he said finally. "Hey. We're still good, right?"

"Huh?"

"I mean, you understand SHA's doing its best, working to get it right?"

"Thanks, Mr. Strahan."

He hung up and I dialed Matt at work. "I confess that I don't know much about anything, but it's not exactly illegal for a developer to put pressure on a government agency, is it? It's like lobbying, right? That citizens group that Jim Bonner's involved with—CATH—they're lobbying too, right?"

"Maybe," Matt said. "It depends on how it's being done. CATH is not buying Strahan dinner at a fancy restaurant. And I suspect that was not the only time Strahan's been wined and dined by Duffy."

Chapter Sixteen
Let It Rip

Dog Sleeps

An intruder allegedly snuck past a Doberman pinscher watchdog early Sunday morning and stole $1,000 worth of stereo equipment from an Annapolis residence, according to county police.

"Time for evaluations," Milton announced as he stood in the doorframe of Big Bill's office.

I was getting a little tired of being assaulted every time I walked in the door.

Milton looked around the empty newsroom. "Nora, looks like you're up first. Six months!"

They call me into the captain's quarters and BB motions for me to sit in an oversized bean bag chair decorated with large navy anchors.

"Ahoy, Nora," Big Bill says. "As you know, it's time for your second evaluation, and I just want to declare at the outset that I'm very sorry for being gruff with you sometimes, for, upon reflection, what you are tackling is not easy. You've obviously been trying to cover all bases, investigating deliberately and thoroughly with a mind toward fairness and justice. If it all comes out right, I envision a three-part series that could just win the paper a Pulitzer."

My leg shook a little as I sat on the hard wooden chair facing my editor's desk. Milton sat beside me as Big Bill handed me the form he had filled out on his typewriter. The type was very faint; I held it close to my face, taking a few minutes to read it over.

Now, I couldn't be entirely sure about this without the other evaluation in hand, but I would have sworn this one was EXACTLY the same as the evaluation I'd received at ten weeks. Come on! Not a single distinction? I had to have improved a little. I felt like I had.

"Average" for accuracy, alertness and creativity.

"Average" suitability for job.

"Average" dependence and drive.

"Above average" for friendliness and appearance.

His comments were somewhat different: "Writing skills and productivity improving. Needs to develop speed and story sources. Recommended for salary increment."

I could care less about a raise. I wanted to be above average! And good things take time, I wanted to scream. Good things come to those who stand and wait.

Milton was like a statue beside me, a midshipman at attention.

"Comments, questions, thoughts?" Big Bill asked.

"I'm getting close. You'll see," was all I said. Then I waved the evaluation at them. "And I've only been here five and a half months, you know."

Sean Duffy had made headlines three times in the past. He'd been a defendant in two high-profile lawsuits, which he had settled, and in 1973, he had sued Buddy Gordon for mismanaging a property that was a joint investment. I made copies of the articles, and returned the microfiche to *The Courier's* librarian in exchange for some she had found about the county's potter's field.

This was a burial ground dating from the 1840s that ran alongside Route 2. Strahan maintained that it would cause significant controversy if the burial sites were disrupted. This was an impact of consequence, the first I was aware of that pertained to Route 2, compared to several liabilities associated with construction over Route 3, Strahan's choice. Originally, this burial site was deemed for "strangers," then "foreigners," and finally "indigents or unclaimed bodies." The term derived from the biblical potter's field in the New Testament, the Valley of Hinnom, from which potting clay was extracted.

Reading about it reminded me of what I most enjoyed about being a reporter: how you became a specialist on subjects you'd never even heard of before.

While my assignments frequently put me on Route 2, and I'd passed it countless times, I had never really taken in Lord's Cemetery before—except to reflexively hold my breath every time I drove by. Jake and I had always held our breath when we passed cemeteries. "Lest a terrible plague befalls thee," he used to joke. A daydreamer, I'd been fortunate that Jake remembered to give me a heads up when a cemetery was imminent. When he forgot to do so, he would take an extra loud inhale and tap me on the shoulder, indicating the cemetery with his head and hoping I caught on before too much bad luck seeped in.

Parking along the shoulder the other day, I had found the site mysterious and inspiring. After some stores, gas stations, and a rare mile of long, lean, trees that Matt would know the name of, it was revealed: an expanse of land covered with rows and rows of low stone markers, looking like endless lines of type. The austere, slate-gray markers were maybe a foot tall, and half as wide, engraved numbers their only memorial.

I now learned that these thirty-four acres (or approximately thirteen hectares, as Walt Strahan would insist on saying) were, to this day, maintained by the Department of Corrections, which bused in prisoners to dig and maintain the graves.

If they dug it up, what *would* SHA do with all those bones? Strahan was right to say this mattered.

I turned in the last of the microfiche, thankful that *The Courier*'s archives were in the basement, making it easy to avoid Connor. I hadn't stopped thinking of him since our last encounter, nice things like the time he had taken me to see *The Deer Hunter* and hadn't teased me for being a wimp, not even for spending ten minutes in the lobby during the Russian roulette scene.

As I walked to the stairwell, I noticed Big Bill talking intently to Roger, *The Courier*'s managing editor, at a table in the corner. Sensing my presence, Big Bill looked up and stopped talking. I smiled and waved, but he just shook his head, his expression unreadable. Oh-kay.

"What the hell!" The front end of my car was sagging, and the tire on the driver's side was flatter than I'd ever seen one, which it hadn't been when I parked this morning. I walked around the back of the car, noticing many dings and scratches that I didn't believe were all my handiwork either. I was terrible at parallel parking, but still. I loved my license plate, UFP15N, and had devised a mnemonic device for remembering it: UFP, Unidentified Flying Person; 15, two days after my birthday; and N for yours truly.

The left rear tire was worn from all the curbs I had distractedly slammed into during my daily roaming—and now I saw that the rear tire on the passenger's side was also flat, with a deep, long gouge in it.

Someone slashed my tires??! @#$%!

"Dammit!" I screamed, a sharp pain streaking through my head. Someone could get in a hell of a lot of trouble for hurting me. I was a newspaper reporter for God's sake!

I jumped into my car, hastily locking all the doors and wishing for the millionth time that my dad had splurged for a model with power windows and locks. There were many cars in this big open lot and from here they all looked untouched. My father had insisted on showing me how to change a tire before I'd left home, but I'd never done it by myself. Besides, there was no way I could change two tires. There weren't even two spares.

Opening the glove compartment for my automobile-club card, I discovered a sheet of paper on top of my notepads, a paper someone else had put there—someone had broken into my car! A new message in the same immature scrawl as before, and again all caps. The words were larger and this time, instead of ink, the alleged perpetrator had used blood or, I reconsidered, a red marker on the verge of drying out.

MINE YUR BIZNES GURLIE

Oh, please! So far-fetched.

But I had to get out of here.

Grasping the note, I ran back inside, down the steps and into the archives. I ran right up to the desk where Big Bill and Roger were still conspiring, shouting at them, "Excuse me, I'm sorry, but look," and I stuffed the sheet of paper into Big Bill's arms, which were casually folded against his chest. "You've got to help me. I need help."

On top of everything else, I had left my AAA card at the scene of the crime.

To say I panicked was an understatement. This was supposed to be a foray into the real world; if I had wanted to become unhinged, I would have joined the Army or Air Force (the Navy always sounded safer somehow). Thank God for Matt. Not only did he know everyone and everything about Anne Arundel County, but he now agreed to be my bodyguard. "Willing and able," he said when I asked, adding, "I still don't think you need to be afraid."

"What will it take?" I asked.

"Someone's just trying to discourage you."

Matt would escort me to and from the paper, where I would restrict my work to phone interviews for the time being. So much for going to the scene.

I spent the first hour of my first day in lockdown writing to Jake. Now that he was lucky in love, I had to initiate all the contact. "I'm writing, not calling, because I want you to give this some thought: Given the ever more 'exciting' circumstances at my job, do you think it's okay to quit?"

At eleven, my phone rang. Buddy Gordon, my Deep Throat, the guy who started all this bisnes [sic].

"I want to applaud you for taking this story seriously," he said. "Seems like you're on the right track now."

"How do you know?"

"Well, you've been talking to Strahan, right?"

"How do you know that?"

"I read your interview. Hey, listen, I have something for you that will help a lot. Can you meet me after work today?"

My stomach churned. "I don't think I can tonight. What is it?"

"Something good, trust me. It will help our side—a lot."

"I'm not on one side or the other. I'm a reporter. I have to stay objective. What do you have?"

"Let me just say, I've done some investigating of my own. I have a source at SHA who has shed light on what's behind the road selection process."

"Will your source meet with me?"

"I've done your homework for you. I have it all on tape. Meet me and I'll give it to you."

I'll give it to you. That was what my dad used to say when he was really mad at Jake.

"Can't you just bring it here to the paper?" I asked.

"Look, I can't be linked to this. We have to meet somewhere else. If it makes you uneasy, you pick the place."

His saying that made me uneasy. "Okay. Let's try for tomorrow night. Call me again tomorrow and I'll tell you when and where."

I called Matt to see if he could take a lunch break.

"Willing and able," he said again. "The Crowd Around Diner?"

"That's fine, but you need to come get me because I don't have my car, because you brought me to work this morning, remember? Because I'm scared to go out alone?"

"Okay, okay, that's right. Take it easy. I'll be there in twenty."

At the nearly empty diner, we requested a booth way in the back, irking the hostess. I recounted my conversation with Buddy.

"Speak louder," Matt kept saying. "There's no one here. And no one could hear you if they were. I'm missing every other word."

"I DON'T WANT TO MEET HIM!" I wrote on my notepad and flicked it toward him. "I'm done with this," I mouthed.

"What?"

"I don't want to do this story anymore," I said in a stage whisper. "And don't tell me I'm crazy."

"Hey, this is why people become reporters," Matt said. "This may be the break you need to rip things open."

"Maybe, but I really don't feel up to it. I'd like to resign now, to tell you the truth."

"Listen, you can do this! I'm going to help you. How did you leave it with Gordon?"

"I told him to call me tomorrow. I wanted us to work out a plan first."

"I've got one. Simple. Meet him here, and I'll be in a booth nearby."

"Really?"

"Why not? Nothing's going to happen, Nora. He just wants to help you break this open, and it sounds like he has something incriminating. What do you think he has?"

"I have no idea."

Linda and Robin both had boyfriends now, so more often than not I spent nights at the house alone. I arranged my schedule so I could get home before dark, and the first thing I did was inspect all the closets and look under all the beds. I left the lights on all night, and slept on the living room couch; if someone came in the back, I'd be out the front door in a second. Linda had gotten some posters framed, which were leaning against the dining room wall, still packaged in brown paper. Strange rustling sounds emanated from those posters, and what sounded like ticking; I unwrapped them to rule out a bomb. Behind the living room drapes, I stationed myself like a legionnaire on a parapet.

I woke up early, really early—it wasn't even morning, but the end of night. I retreated to my bed at last, where I lingered on my back, barely able to discern the outlines of the window across from me, a square window, maybe only two feet by two feet, curtain-less, and situated higher up on the wall than normal, like a window in a prison cell, filled with blackness.

> And I, too, felt ready to start life over again.... [G]azing up at the dark sky spangled with its signs and stars, for the first time, the first, I laid my heart open to the benign indifference of the universe.

The Stranger, by Albert Camus, my all-time favorite book for its deceptive simplicity and major existential angst. I jumped out of bed, turned on the light, threw on a sweatshirt, pulled out my journal, and sat down to write.

Entry #59

The other night, Dad and I talked about how we like the early hours of the day the best: quiet, private, emerging light, and just a few people around to appreciate it. A little later, I called Jake to tell him what was going on down here—unable to wait for him to get my letter—and he said, 'Are you anxious or eager?' 'Both,' I said. 'Well, that's not bad because anxious is worried, but eager is good,' he said. 'I think you should tough it out.'

Buddy showed up at the diner on schedule that evening, but we never went inside. Once again, he was dressed in polyester, and I wondered if he made his own UHF commercials for his real-estate company. He said he needed to play the cassette for me on his car's tape deck. Fortunately, Matt figured it out and soon came out of the diner to wait in his car. He was a few parking spots away, and it was all I could do not to glance in his direction.

"Should I bring Jason's gun—just in case?" Matt had asked that morning, I hoped in jest. He lived with three other guys, two of whom I had met. One of them, whom Matt had known since childhood, was training to be a cop.

"No, no guns," I had said. "Don't you read my crime-prevention columns?"

Although people keep handguns in their homes for security reasons, they are much more likely to kill or injure a family member or friend than an intruder.

The tape Buddy played was his conversation with an engineer who worked directly under Strahan. It was less than a minute long, but the engineer emphatically states that preparations to build on Route 3 were underway. "We have told him [Strahan] repeatedly of potential hazards that need further assessment, but he keeps saying there isn't enough time and we need to push the project through. He keeps saying move ahead."

"Can you prove this?" Buddy asks the engineer.

"We've written a lot of memos."

"Is Strahan being pressured? Is that why he's ignoring your warnings?" Buddy asks.

"There are rumors he's being wined and dined," the engineer says just as the tape cuts off.

"Wow," I said to Buddy. "This is good. Can he get us the memos?"

"I'll ask."

"Can I keep the tape?"

He ejected it and tossed it in my lap, which he then proceeded to stare at.

"Thanks a lot," I said, ejecting myself from his car.

"Hey," he called after me, getting out, too. "Stay in touch now. Keep me in the loop, young lady."

I nodded as I watched him get back in his Cadillac. Inside the diner, I waited for Matt, who came in shortly after Buddy drove off.

"This is great," Matt said after I filled him in. "Wining and dining is good. Now you just need further evidence and further corroboration. He needs to get us the memos."

It was hard not to be affected by Matt's relentless enthusiasm. He spoke—at all times—with the intensity that the rest of us saved for job interviews. He gesticulated a lot, and his eyes grew bigger and bigger as he made his points.

"Well, I can only plow ahead if I'm not freaking out the entire time about my safety," I said. I paused and clenched my teeth. "Please don't get the wrong idea, but do you think I could move in with you and the guys for awhile?"

Matt's face brightened and I felt a sharp pang of guilt. "We'd be delighted to harbor you," he said. "By the way, have I mentioned Jason has a gun?"

Chapter Seventeen
Hullabaloo

Cold Case

Responding to Jaegar's Seafood Shoppe in Glen Burnie at 6:30 Tuesday night, county police arrested Mike Hudson, 38, of Potomac, who allegedly was discovered in the stand-up freezer stuffing frozen lobster tails down his pants.

The senior engineer was not aware that Buddy had taped him, and he was very concerned about remaining anonymous. When he refused to leak agency memos, I asked Buddy to ask him if someone else would be willing. Shortly after my request, I received a call from Gene Black, another engineer working on the freeway project. We arranged to meet at the Burger King on Richie Highway.

Since Matt had to work, I enlisted Robin to accompany me to this meeting. As a waitress, her days were free, so she liked to sleep in. Well, I could work around that. Robin was petite, offering as much protection as a Chihuahua, but she was another live body, and I reasoned it had to be harder to abduct two people than one.

I wasn't sure I was supposed to do this, but I bought Engineer Black a Whopper and Coke, and Robin fries, after which we slid into a booth near the bathrooms. I placed my cassette recorder in the center of the table; the few other patrons were in fast food heaven, unconscious. "Hope you're okay with my taping this conversation?" I asked.

"Okay with me," Gene said. "Truthfully, I'm happy this is going to be publicized because what's going on is downright wrong. It comes down to this: Time and again, Strahan has dismissed our reservations and pleas to delay building the road over Route 3 until further investigation is done. Some of our findings and recommendations never saw the light of day. They definitely never made it into the environmental reports SHA showed the public at those so-called hearings. If the road is constructed over Route 3, it could be a nightmare."

"A nightmare?" Robin asked, tearing herself away from her fries.

"There's a few nightmares actually," Gene said. "But Strahan won't listen. He's on a mission and keeps saying our concerns would take too long to explore, and that they're overblown."

"What are your concerns?" I asked.

"Here's a giant red flag. Excavation to expand Route 3 could result in the reopening of a landfill in Stockville that was problematic to begin with. The aquifer could be contaminated, compromising the drinking supply. It could be very serious."

"Groundwater contamination?" I hadn't seen anything about that, but I had this queasy feeling that way back Major Keating had mentioned something about the water supply.

"Yes—that needs to come out soon. The suspicion is that this landfill was not closed correctly back in the day. And we're not sure of the implications of reopening it. Disturbing it could cause the release of contaminants, not to mention it could cost a fortune to close it properly this time. That's what I mean by nightmare."

"Your boss, Strahan, has told me that there's great concern about the potter's field that would have to be excavated if the road were built over Route 2."

"Not at all the same thing," Gene said.

"I wondered because I recently drove by there, and it seems like the nearest graves are at least fifty feet from the road, so would they have to be disturbed at all?"

Gene Black applauded me like I'd just won a round of Jeopardy. "That's exactly right. You're talking about maybe disturbing a few rows of graves versus the drinking supply for many towns. Route 2 is the better choice all around. The potter's field situation is manageable."

"Even though people can be weird about cemeteries," I said. "Wow. Can I ask you something else? Are the stakes and pipes—and tractors—I've seen along Route 3 in preparation for building the highway?"

Gene shook his head up and down, pleased that I knew about these, too. "You've done your research. Preparations have been underway since the fall. Groundbreaking could occur in as little as a few weeks, if the weather continues to warm."

Eureka. On a roll. Now for the bonus round. "Do you know if the developer Sean Duffy is influencing Strahan's decision?" I asked.

For the first time, Gene looked uncomfortable. He asked me to stop the tape. Buddy had told me the first, anonymous engineer was an older man, whereas Gene was maybe in his early thirties. It was surprising that he was willing to put his neck on the line. "Strictly off the record, I would look into that," he said, his voice hushed. "Dining. Ball games. Junkets."

"We're going to need documentation," I said. "The findings about the landfill, memos, studies that should have been made public, but weren't. Everything you can put your hands on—especially some memos."

The youngish engineer stood up and we all shook hands. "I'll see what I can do."

Delegate Jim Bonner was dumbfounded when I played the engineers' tapes for him. "The wining and dining is one thing, but the fact that they're saying building is about to begin is monumental," he said. "The implication is that the public hearings were a sham."

"And that potential hazards are being ignored," I added. "And information withheld."

"I'll need to speak to the chairman of the transportation committee," Bonner said. "I'll get back to you shortly. We'll have to act fast."

At Matt's house that evening, I told him I'd screwed up a bit. "My session with Gene ended abruptly when I asked if he thought Duffy was bribing Strahan—not in those words, Matt! I don't think I found out everything he meant when he said there were nightmares with the Route 3 option."

"Well, a toxic landfill is a big deal. Anyway, I don't think you have to worry. Sounds like Bonner will take care of the interviewing from here. He sits on the Transportation and Public Works Committee, but he needs the chairman to issue the subpoenas."

"What are the subpoenas for?" I asked, tired of my ignorance and ever grateful that at least one of us had read newspapers regularly while growing up, and could shed some light.

"The subpoenas will force SHA and its engineers to produce all of their work project records and memos, all internal communications and all studies. Soliciting the info via subpoenas helps protect the engineers, like that first guy who wanted to be kept out of it."

"He's going to be very unhappy if he's subpoenaed."

"They may not need him. But if he's called, it will be because of his seniority. It won't be evident that he talked."

When I updated Big Bill on all that had happened, he was the happiest I'd seen him since my arrival at the newspaper. "Well done," he said. "Now we're talking."

With Bonner on the case, I knew I had to get to Duffy fast. Because Gene Black had said road construction could start any day, there was only a small window of time before the State House hearings would begin. As soon as they were set, my first article would come out, and then there was no way the kingpin of Duffy Development would agree to see me.

Although his secretary was always cordial on the phone, she had kept postponing our appointments. So with Robin in tow, I drove to the company's headquarters in Alexandria, Virginia.

As it happened, Duffy was speaking to his secretary in the reception area when we arrived. He squinted at me, perhaps recalling our brief encounter at the restaurant that time, but he consented to sit down with me for a few minutes. Robin followed us into his office. "She's our new intern," I said.

Duffy was handsome and polite, and again tastefully dressed. The contrast with Buddy Gordon was dramatic. In a switcheroo, he announced that he would be taping everything we said, removing a fancy recording device from a shelf and setting it up. "You must have just finished college," he began. Warming *me* up?

"I graduated last year."

"And how old can *you* be?" he asked Robin in a condescending tone.

"I'm thinking of following in her footsteps," she said, chuckling.

Robin was good-natured and brave, at nineteen still imbued with that feeling young people are supposed to have that they're invincible, whereas at twenty-three, I knew better. At sixteen, her mother had kicked her out of the house when she got pregnant, and she'd dropped out of school. It was a shame because she was smart and had a good sense about things, sometimes posing interesting questions.

Duffy, who seemed to be taking notes himself, returned to me. "Let me ask you something. I know you've talked with Walt Strahan several times, so why would you need to speak to me? What has Strahan said about our meetings?"

"Well, I understand you've been following the hearings for the new freeway, I-97, quite closely and that you have a lot of land that would benefit from it being built over Route 3. Is that right?"

"Yes, we do own land along Route 3 and have two projects in mind, one ready to go."

"One of them is that mega complex in Severna Park, right? What exactly are you building there?"

"It's mixed use, very exciting. Townhouses, commercial space for offices, retail stores, and entertainment—as well as green spaces. It will generate about five thousand new jobs and be a tremendous boost to the whole county."

"What kind of entertainment?" Robin asked.

"We have interest in a few restaurants, and a movie complex with eight theaters."

"Great!" Robin said, and I glared at her.

"But what about the environmental hazards that could result from building the highway on Route 3?" I asked.

"There are always impacts when developing land. These are run-of-the-mill, is my understanding."

"I don't know if you have actually been to the State Highway Authority's public forums, but there are a lot of people who are against the highway being built on Route 3. They're worried about the upheaval and more congestion, as well as the potential for serious harm."

"The SHA will ensure that any harm is kept to a minimum. The aim is to improve the roads *and* the land. The congestion will get better, and as your intern just said, this is great for the community! Some people just don't like change," Duffy said.

"I understand there's a landfill near Stockville that could become unstable if Route 3 is used. That could end up contaminating the drinking water for everyone in that area. If that happens, would your company be prepared to absorb the costs of rectifying it?"

"That's overblown. Strahan has assured me that landfill's fine," Duffy said, starting to fidget.

"Mr. Strahan has said you are very good friends. How long have you known him?"

Duffy stared at me.

"What do you discuss about the highway project when you dine together?" I asked.

"I have been pushing for the Route 3 option. As I said, it would bring many jobs and much revenue."

"How much do these dinners cost?"

Duffy smacked off the tape recorder and rose from his chair, saying, "None of your business. We are friendly, but there is absolutely nothing untoward going on."

I got up, too, while underlining that quote; in my opinion, it was just the kind of thing a guilty man would say. And "overblown" was also an interesting word choice, since that was what Gene had quoted Strahan saying—about everything. I pulled Robin with me toward the door, which was shut. "When I ran into you with Walter Strahan at Beau Rivage, you picked up the check," someone in my body said as I turned the door knob.

Duffy waved us away, like he was flicking away flies. "That's enough. Case closed. End of conversation."

My first piece about the highway brouhaha appeared on the front page of both newspapers with a banner headline.

Superhighway Project Investigated

By Nora Plowright
Staff Writer

The House of Delegates has convened a special panel to investigate possible wrongdoing by the State Highway Authority (SHA) in its handling of plans and public hearings for a possible new freeway, I-97, intended to run from Baltimore to south of Severna Park.

"We are looking into whether the highway administration's decision was made with disregard to opinions solicited at public hearings," Delegate James E. Bonner (D), District 47, stated.

The transportation committee had subpoenaed the memos of the key SHA engineers, including both of my sources. Over and over, they warned that the project was underway, but should not proceed, at least not along Route 3, until certain issues were investigated further and resolved satisfactorily.

Gene Black testified before the House of Delegates' panel. He provided damaging documentation, in particular about the landfill.

Matt came with me to the first hearing at the State House in Annapolis, where we met up with Megan Best, who would co-write the next articles with me since the House of Delegates was her beat.

"By the way, I heard from Yale and Northwestern," Matt said.

"So, how'd you do?"

He looked sheepish. "I got in."

"Wow, that's fantastic, Matt. You'll go to Yale, right? What about the others?"

"That's all I've heard from so far. Not sure what I'll do. I have time to decide."

"You're going to make a terrific lawyer," I said. "In a way, you've been my attorney for months. I'd love to take you out to celebrate, and thank you for all the help you've given me. All of this wouldn't be taking place if it weren't for you, and I know a few nice restaurants, too, now."

Matt smiled. "It's been a lot of fun."

He also seemed to have fun sitting between me and Megan, who was attractive and fashionable. A few years older than us, she had been at *The Courier* for two years. She was business-like with me, laying down the rules for our collaboration: "If it's okay, I'll write the first draft, then you can elaborate on the details and make sure everything's accurate." Fine with me.

We spent the next several weeks at the State House, posting pieces every few days. When he could, Matt attended the hearings, and we always sat girl/boy/girl. He paid a lot of attention to Megan. It would be nice if he had a fling with her, I thought, although I felt a tad rejected. I was still sleeping on the pull-out couch in his living room, and he wasn't around much of late. Most nights, I watched sports with his housemates.

But it was novel for me to have a bonanza of stories, all appearing on the top of the front page and culminating with this bombshell:

Will a Superhighway Cut Through North County?

By Nora Plowright and Megan Best
Staff Writers

A band of citizens, led by members of Citizens Against the Highway (CATH), have filed for an injunction to halt construction preparations for I-97, a proposed six-lane freeway, on the grounds that the project was not adequately investigated, that environmental impacts were not fully assessed and others ignored, and that certain studies were withheld from the public.

The day this piece ran, I also had a sidebar about rookie delegate Bonner and the dogged citizens behind CATH. My reporting and related photos took up the entire front page of both *The Record* and *The Courier.*

I was the star of my newsroom. Everyone huddled around me once again, at last not because of a gaffe I had committed.

Two pink "While you were out" message slips were propped up on my typewriter. One was from Delegate Bonner, asking me to call; the other from Walter Strahan. This was Strahan's message: "We're still good, right?"

This was too hard. I'd been hoping all the hoopla—especially the injunction against the highway—was enough, but now Bonner told me he was deep into pursuing impropriety between Strahan and Duffy. "You'll be seeing them soon at our hearings," he said, which gave me the willies. It was getting too personal.

Big Bill was dismayed when, later that afternoon, I told him I wanted to be taken off the highway story. "I've brought it this far, but that's it for me."

"But you broke the story. You've done all the legwork. Why don't you want to continue? Because of those silly notes?" he asked, that mysterious expression of his returning.

"I guess I have an overdeveloped sense of self-preservation," I said. "I'm happy to go back to features. This is getting too exciting."

"But what about Duffy? There's still more to come out. *Please,*" Big Bill said. "Just finish what you've started with Duffy."

"I'm willing to help out behind the scenes, but I don't want anyone to know I'm still involved. No more bylines for me on this business."

"It doesn't make sense. If you want, I'll have Catherine assist you."

Ugh. "I feel strongly about this," I said.

"I'm happy to write the articles with you," Catherine told me later. "And I'm more than happy to share the bylines with you, no matter how much you do. After all, this has always been your story, and Bonner is your beat."

I appreciated her heightened respect. "Aren't you worried about the threats?" I asked. "Why haven't people taken them more seriously?"

"I'm not worried at all," she replied. "Whoever did that was trying to prevent the story from coming out. Now that it has, what can they do?"

When I started to walk away, she called me back. "Gee whiz, I just can't comprehend why you'd quit the story now. This is the good part, the big payday."

I shrugged. Even if Catherine used expressions like "gee whiz" and "holy cow," she could never understand that I felt somewhat sorry for Strahan and Duffy, and what they were about to go through.

I organized my notes and all of the documents I'd collected, including my interviews with Strahan and Duffy. I had done what I'd set out to do, and was proud of myself for taking things this far, for being the catalyst in uncovering corruption. It was harder than I would have expected to give up my brief brush with celebrity; I had enjoyed the recognition I'd received with each new byline on this story. But I was relieved to leave the rest to the others, and didn't need any more credit. I had jabbed my hockey stick in there for awhile, but now I wanted to rest on the bench. I was plenty happy now to *go gently into that good night*. Plus, I had other plans.

Big Bill gave me a reprieve from deadlines in exchange for putting together a series about Stockville, "the town a railroad built," which is something he had wanted to publish for a long time, requiring many interviews and some research. All of my favorite characters would be included: General Westbrook, the volunteer paramedics, Mayor Keating, the town historian. I set to work. And I moved back to the house on Carroll Drive.

A few weeks later, the Strahan/Duffy drama broke.

Was the SHA Bribed?
Head Highway Engineer Investigated

By Megan Best and Catherine Dodson
Staff Writers

After a review of credit card statements of the real-estate firm Duffy Development Inc., the Maryland

House Transportation Committee has charged that funds were used inappropriately to sponsor extravagant weekends in Washington, D.C., and an all-expenses-paid junket to the Cayman Islands for the top State Highway Authority (SHA) engineer.

For these perks, along with Baltimore Colts season tickets and frequent use of an "escort service," Strahan had been willing to ignore all kinds of warnings and place a road where Duffy stood to make a fortune.

He had the audacity to call me. "What the hell is wrong with you? You sold me down the river. I tried to work with you."

"Did you write those threatening notes, Mr. Strahan? Did you have my tires slashed?"

"What in the world are you talking about? Surely, I don't seem like someone who would do that!"

Calls came in, readers wanting to weigh in on corruption and injustice. "It just figures," ran the common sentiment. Earlier in the decade, the county executives of both Anne Arundel and Baltimore County had been indicted, and Spiro Agnew, Maryland's first Vice President, had been nailed for tax fraud.

"No surprise that no President has ever hailed from the Great State of Maryland," I said to Milton.

"Oh, you're such a snob," he said. "People make fun of 'Joisey' too, you know."

When my three-part series on Stockville was finished, I felt proud, the way I always felt at the end of finals. I turned it all in, along with my written resignation from *The Anne Arundel Record*.

Big Bill looked at the piece of paper, then me, in utter disbelief. He looked crestfallen. "Is this a joke?" he asked. "Why would you leave now? You got your wish—I took you off the story. And I can tell you enjoyed doing this series. You're just starting to get the hang of it. It turns out you have good instincts and are surprisingly tenacious."

"Thanks," I said, taken aback by this display of praise. "I appreciate that. And great to leave on a high note."

Silence.

"The biggest thing, you know, is that my parents need me to—" I started to lie, then stopped myself. "Actually, the biggest thing is that this isn't for me. I want to be a writer, but not a reporter. Every time someone says something, I want to change it, improve it, make it more interesting. I'm so tempted to embellish people's quotes, add livelier details—"

"What?" Big Bill said with alarm.

"But I don't do it! I always come back to the conventional, blasé truth."

> Many more citizens than were expected crowded the governor's mansion Thursday at a birthday dinner for the two oldest ladies in Anne Arundel County.

"Also, you know I don't love confronting people."

"Don't sell yourself short," BB said. "Listen, I appreciate how you feel, but you can always write fiction later—this will give you endless material. I think it's just a crying shame." I could see his mood darken. "You should know that if you leave, it will have serious consequences, at least if you ever want to work in journalism again, if you change your mind. It won't be easy to get back in."

"I know," I said.

"Personally, I think you should give it more thought, sleep on it, maybe a few nights," my editor said.

"But—"

"Will you do that for me?"

I strode out to the paper's parking lot, that same scary lot where I found the first threatening note on a cold, bleak night in January. The grass needed a trim, but pretty pansies lined the walk. It was still light, and the sky was clear, visibility 100 percent.

I was 90 percent fear-free and felt an enormous sense of relief as I got into my car. I was not one to regret decisions—that was my credo—and I felt sure of myself here. Follow your dreams, my father had taught. I was so lucky to have the luxury to try.

Chapter Eighteen
Spring Back

Woman Dies after Saving Family

A 40-year-old Severna Park woman shoved her father out of their burning home and carried her two young children to safety before dying when she returned to the house in an attempt to save the cat, county fire officials reported.

Catherine's wedding was sort of my going away party, and the weather was splendid: cloudless skies, sunny and warm, no humidity. The day before, I had written my last police blurbs, packed up my desk at the newsroom, and uncharacteristically spent the afternoon clothes shopping: a dramatic red silk dress, black heels, a new pocketbook, and more adventurous blush. "You're so pretty. Show it off," my mom liked to tell me. I liked to tease her by saying I felt like a female impersonator when I dressed up.

The ceremony was at a Catholic church replete with gold statues and exquisite stained glass. "*I like the silent church before the service begins better than any preaching*," I whispered to Milton, who had found me in the pews.

"Martin Luther King?" he whispered back. "e e cummings?"

What was with e e cummings? "Good try," I said. "Emerson. Ralph Waldo."

"None of us knew you wanted to go back to school," Milton said.
"Yeah, I know. It all came together fast."

After giving notice, I had spent two weeks hearing everyone's reactions to my leaving:

- Big Bill, eyes on work: "So, you're really going?"
  "I got into Stanford's creative writing program. They'll let me start this summer."
  Looking up at last: "Graduate School? Congratulations. Can't argue with that."

- Matt: "I've got a surprise for you, too."
  "You're dating Megan."
  "No—close, I'm dating one of her friends. But that's not it. I'm deferring law school. I'm going to work at *The Courier* for a year instead. They're giving me the courthouse beat."

- Jack: "You've only been here two minutes!"
  "I have to tell you, police beat was the best part of my day, despite the horror."
  "Well, lots of luck, girlie."

MINE YUR BIZNES GURLIE

Nah.

At one point during the service, Catherine's mother led her into a small chapel off the main pulpit so they could pray privately to the Virgin Mary. I watched Mark watch his bride with her mom in the little room. His eyes never left her. They had met on her second day at *The Record*, when Mark was still at *The Courier*. Allegedly, they both knew instantly this was it. "We'd both kissed a lot of frogs," Catherine had said.

Now standing sideways, facing each other, the bride and groom were bathed in light, like actors on a stage about to break into song. Still, whenever I looked at Catherine, finally a size 10, I couldn't help picturing the flasher at her kitchen window.

The wedding mass wasn't interminable and the celebration began at one at "The Sanctuary," a catering hall in Jessup that boasted at least a hectare of richly landscaped grounds. Milton gave me a ride over. "You okay being my date?" I asked, fishing for compliments.

"Happy to oblige, me lady," he answered.

We were to spend the entire afternoon outside, and before I ate anything, I acquired a martini that was super strong. The tumblers were decorated with palm tree stickers. Catherine loved palm trees. She had a few plastic palm trees on her office desk.

Milton tapped me on the left shoulder and I swung around only to find him on my right. He loved playing games like this.

"Lovely affair, don't you know, what?" he said.

I smiled.

"I'm sure going to miss your big smile when you come in every morning, Nora."

"I have to say, it's been a good run. I've learned a lot."

"Try this. It's a Singapore Sling."

I took a big sip. "Love this!"

"Keep it. I'll get another. Be right back."

As I guzzled the sweet drink, the sun bore down on me. I grabbed two pigs in blankets when the tray passed by, one for Milton, who returned with a gigantic new drink for us to share and a little purple cocktail umbrella tucked in his hair.

"Wanna dance?" he asked.

"I only slow dance." The band was playing "Lady Godiva," which was way too zippy.

"I'll get us some snacks. Right back," Milton said. He was revved up today.

I polished off the two drinks I was holding, my mouth filling with baby ice cubes. Some liquid trickled down onto my new dress.

"Nice party," Big Bill said, coming up behind me. "Pretty dress."

"Hell, yes," I said, dribbling the ice back into the glass. "Oops. 'Scuse me. I was referring to the party, not my dress. I—"

"So, what kind of stuff do you like to write?" my editor asked.

"Might try my hand at a novel," I said. I had submitted two short stories with my applications, one about an epiphany at a very tense family dinner, the other about a young, naive reporter who writes an article about a beloved town hero who turns out to be a pedophile.

"Good luck with that!" BB said sardonically. He shifted his weight from one leg to the other, back and forth. "I love mysteries myself."

"Not sure they would be my strong suit," I said. In my college creative writing workshops, everyone had wanted me to make my villains more nefarious. Something to work on.

"Well, I should get back to my wife. Just wanted to say good-bye again, and wish you luck, and thank you for your efforts. I *knew* Duffy was in on this fix, I would have sworn to it, but I didn't think he'd stoop to this. Although why should I be surprised? He's always been devious and self-serving, a slimy son of a gun."

"I didn't know you knew him."

"I have the dubious honor of being his half brother. I know him all too well."

AAAAH!!! For a second, I considered whether Big Bill was pulling my leg, but it was clear from the look of contempt on his face that he was being straight.

"Took you long enough to get to the bottom of this," he continued. "It was an uphill battle keeping you motivated. Heh-heh."

Did he really just say "heh-heh"? His tone, which had sounded bitter and angry as he described Duffy, now sounded downright evil. He winked at me in a disturbing way. Where was Milton with those drinks?

"Oh well. Best of luck to you, Nora. Keep in touch." As he pecked my cheek, I smelled the salty sea on his skin, and my Pavlovian response was to feel a tight, figure-eight knot form in my stomach.

I pushed through the crowd, searching for Catherine-the-bride, because I had to see if she knew Duffy and Big Bill were related, and was this relevant? I couldn't think it through. Big Bill had withheld this detail when he kept coaxing me to follow the moneyed interests. And he had acted so put out whenever my probing stalled, when I couldn't find my way. I had thought he was spurring me on as my editor, but clearly he'd had his own agenda. I pictured him that afternoon with Roger at *The Courier*, the afternoon my tires were slashed.

And suddenly I got it: *He* did it, Big Bill, my wise, trusted counselor. Either did it himself or had ordered it done. Perhaps he'd also been stalking me, trying to motivate me through fear to tie the loose ends together and produce the story already, revenge against his half brother, whom he despised.

I walked briskly in circles around the vast grounds, bumping into all these women dressed in white even though it wasn't their wedding. And it wasn't Memorial Day yet either, and I was pretty sure there was a fashion rule about not wearing white until then.

Did Big Bill write those absurd, threatening notes?

There was a big dark splotch on my new red dress, which I hoped was alcohol, not grease.

Would BB really do that? Were the notes his way of signaling that I was on the right track?

Just because you think something doesn't make it true, my father would say.

Besides, why would BB think frightening me would be motivating?

At a neglected cocktail station on the fringe of the grounds, I ordered a Tom Collins, resolving to try as many different drinks today as possible.

"Tom or Bud?" the goofy bartender joked.

"That's funny," I said, stumbling away and colliding with Mark, the groom, my newest drink splashing over both of us.

"I had that coming," he said.

"You did!" I said.

"Although that was kind of outrageous, your following me to my house."

"Well, here you are in the flesh. I've finally caught up with you, and at your wedding no less! Unbelievable. Thank you for fitting me in. I've wanted to interview you for, what, half a year? So many things I wanted to ask you about the county exec."

He punched me in the shoulder, a little too hard. "Haven't you heard? I resigned, effective last Monday."

Like me, Mark had had a lot to drink, and maybe not even one pig-in-a-blanket. Where were the other hors d'oeuvres?

"And by the way, I didn't quit just because of the stuff that's been in the news—Pascarelli's fun at the county's expense," Mark said, "although it burned me that I was the last to know about that." He moved close to whisper in my ear, which tickled, but I stayed still. "Turns out my boss is involved with Duffy too. He investigated Buddy Gordon years ago on a Sean Duffy tip. They're thick as thieves. And no doubt he was also availing himself of girls, girls, girls! He'll be tied to this too. You'll see."

Unbelievable all the dirt I was getting that I wouldn't be able to use. Unbelievable what could happen when you totally stopped trying.

Mark put his index finger over my lips. "Can't tell Catherine about this," he slurred. "She's getting warm anyhow, but she has to find out on her own. It can't come from me."

I opened my mouth—

"Hush. You know what? From now on I'm staying clear of papers and politicians, especially Pascarelli," he said, spitting out the "P's." "No more 'p' careers for me."

"Me too," I said.

"Thinking of working in a bike shop. I love bikes," he said.

"Catherine's looking for you, Mark," Milton said, holding a tray waiter-style, high above his head. Small plates of Swedish meatballs and shrimp toast—and a strawberry daiquiri.

"All I could carry. We can share." He jabbed a green cocktail umbrella into my scalp.

"Ouch. Give Mark some of those. Where's Catherine?"

"They're taking more pictures. She looks fantastic."

"She's lost so much weight." Catherine had recently told me that she used to eat entire Sara Lee cakes in her car on her way home from work.

We sat on the lush grass on the outskirts of the party, partially shaded from the heat by a large hedge. I wanted to tell Milton what I'd learned, but I knew these men had confided in me off the record and out of some profound trust based on their knowledge that I was leaving, heading off to other worlds directly after this party.

"So, I just heard something interesting," Milton said. "Apparently, that young engineer—the one who testified? He's leaving the SHA to work for Buddy's development company."

"Gene Black. Here's to Gene!" I said, raising one of my glasses. "Let's talk about something else."

We actually didn't talk at all for a time. It was peaceful sitting side by side on the grass. Milton's shoulder pressed into me slightly, and I tugged the hem of my dress over my knees. Then, even though the band was still doing "fast" songs, Milton yanked me to my feet and I let him pull me over to the raised dance floor. His gyrations made me laugh, and when he sang along, *I'm gonna getcha getcha getcha getcha*, I laughed so hard that I didn't have to dance. I just stood there laughing while he put on a show. Soon the band segued into "Can't Help Falling in Love," and he held his arms out.

Milton had always been nice to me. I put my arms around him, but in heels I was about three inches taller, so I crouched in order to rest my head on his shoulder as he pulled me in snugly, just the way we used to dance at bar mitzvahs. I was having the same tingly feelings I'd had then, and when the song finished, Milton took my hand and led me inside the catering hall, where it was twenty degrees cooler, to a private bathroom he had scoped out. Inside, he locked the door, and I giggled, although I was dizzy. Milton drew me to him and kissed me, and I kissed him back, scrunching down, and we kissed and kissed, the way people only did when they were really drunk or really high. I held him tight, partly so I wouldn't fall because I was so light-headed, but then he touched my breasts, squeezing my nipples, and I knew it was all over for me, that I was gone, and he spread his jacket out on the carpet and pulled me down on top of him, and it was okay, this once…

When we were dressed again and standing by the entrance of an open-air tent, which guests were streaming into for the late luncheon, I felt shy. Why did I just do that? "I can't stay. I have to get going," I said to the grass.

"No, don't go yet," Milton said, gently lifting my chin with his hand so that I had to look at him. "You know, I never thanked you for calling me Milton."

I smiled and gave him a quick kiss. "I have to leave. Catherine will understand. No one has a clue what goes on at their wedding."

Milton touched my bare arm. "I've dreamt of this since the first day we met."

I shook my head and laughed. "Oh, I bet you say that to all the girls. Can you drop me back at the church?"

The night before, I never slept. At five a.m., I embarked on a drive, retracing all the routes of my tenure: Route 3, Route 2, Route 100, country lanes and back roads whose names were still unknown to me, partly because of the paucity of signage. I had driven in the blackness at that most eerie time when demons lurk, fully facing my fears at last.

The fog had been thick as I drove over the Old Bay Bridge into Annapolis, past Connor's garden apartment, past *The Courier*, through the quaint, historic town. I drove past Matt's house and past *The Record*. The night was dark, the silence deep. The early morning fog seemed dreamy, like a layer of linen. At night, it made your sense of isolation more complete.

My belongings had been packed for more than a week, and after Linda and Robin helped me load the car, we had sat in the breakfast room together one last time.

"We're gonna miss you," Linda said. "And now you're going to miss our annual Fourth of July party."

Robin was quiet, mad at me for leaving.

"I have something for you, Robin." From a thick manila envelope, I pulled out pamphlets, brochures, and catalogs I'd gathered for her—for acquiring a GED, for the local adult ed school, for Anne Arundel Community College and the University of Maryland.

She took the stack from me, wiping her eyes as we hugged.

Before getting onto the highway, I stopped at Brady's and forced down a tuna-salad sandwich and coffee. My head was splitting from the assortment of mixed drinks. The counter was filled with people, local people like those I had written about, people who subscribed to *The Anne Arundel Record*.

How arbitrary it all was: who I wrote about, what I wrote. Who I met, who I thought to call, who answered their phones, what they chose to tell me. What I thought to ask them next, what I didn't fully comprehend, what I completely missed or left out. "Just the facts, ma'am," they said, but it was just the facts that you elicited, and then just the ones you chose to include.

As a parting gesture, I picked up the Saturday *Courier*.

Pascarelli Linked To SHA Scandal

By Connor Aloysius Hannah
Staff Writer

So many times during the last few weeks, I had picked up the phone to call Connor, then stopped. The article described a new investigation by the House of Delegates into whether Pascarelli's chief of staff had exerted pressure on Bonner to stop delving into the highway story—and whether Pascarelli knew about it.

> "Regrettably, large sums of money connected to development have been known to breed corruption among appointed, and even elected, officials," State Delegate James E. Bonner (D), District 47, said.

I realized with a pang that I had forgotten to tell Bonner I was leaving, but I couldn't do anything about that now. Instead, I used the pay phone to call Connor, not confident it was the right move, but happy for a last opportunity to say goodbye.

"Nora? I thought you left."

"I'm taking off now, but I just saw today's paper. How long have you known about Pascarelli?"

"Oh, a little while. I wanted to let your news break first."

"You mean you not only buried a lead, but a whole story?" I asked.

"Ladies first," he said softly. "Lots of luck, Nora. Good luck with everything."

I sighed, involuntarily placing my hand over my heart like I was about to say the "Pledge of Allegiance." I was not one to have regrets, but maybe I had missed the boat with Connor.

Back in my car, I waited at a red light and when it turned green, the woman in the car ahead just sat there. One, two, three—I pressed my horn. At this, the lady sped off, and within seconds, she was traveling well over the speed limit. Was she determined to put as much distance between us as possible? Or show me she was not a slacker after all? She was going so fast now that she nearly rear-ended the pick-up truck in front of her. Was she trying to say, "Hey, I can be aggressive!" or "I'm the worst driver ever"?

And there you had it. I didn't need to be a reporter to write about people and their lives. I could say so much more with time to reflect and flesh out my characters, not composing in a whirlwind to meet a deadline every few days. So often I'd had to settle for a snapshot of a story. If a teenage girl was shot and her neighbors claimed she was good and never got into trouble, we went with that, satisfied with the ready explanation: The boy next door had been fooling around with his father's hunting rifle. But who knew what either of those kids had really been up to? Maybe she had been taunting him for years? Maybe he had been threatening her for longer?

As I crossed into Delaware, I realized I'd left pieces of myself behind: my favorite nightgown at Connor's, some books at Matt's, my few items of furniture with Linda and Robin. Many, many newspaper clips.

I was driving home to my folks, but in my big, old, tired car, I felt unsettled. Though you wrote about people all the time, to be a reporter was to spend hours and hours wandering around, followed by the solitary writing. I had spent a lifetime in my car, it seemed, and while it had conveyed me to interviews with many people in myriad situations, day after day, it still was a lonely line of work. Of course, writing in graduate school would have its lonely moments as well.

The late afternoon sun struck me through the trees, smacked me in my aching head, flashing at me as I traveled up the long road. I remembered my parents trying to teach me to swim, begging me to put my head under water. They had stood beside me in the lake at our summer bungalow community as other kids jumped off the dock, leaping with joy and splashing water in my face with their cannonballs. It was another story my mother liked to tell; she found it charming. "They're flashing, you'd say. They're flashing. Make them stop flashing." I found it embarrassing—but, hey, I could say the word "splashing" now. And I could stick my head under water now too!

For the ride home, I had a special treat. For fifty-nine cents, I'd bought a bag of assorted "puffs," which I dumped out onto the passenger seat. They resembled soft peppermints, white with stripes, only instead of red, the stripes were various colors, purportedly lemon, cherry, grape, orange, lime, and cream. Each flavor was worse than the one before, 100 percent artificial, and soon my teeth were streaked with the whole palette, my tongue a dark purple. Still, I popped them out of their wrappers and chewed them rapidly, the car filling with a cloying odor.

Catherine Dolby has three children in four years and is now a Weight Watchers leader.

Milton becomes a regional editor at The Baltimore Sun, *eventually rising to managing editor. He marries a former NCAA gymnast.*

Sean Duffy receives fifteen years in jail, and Big Bill retires from The Record *to become president of Duffy Development.*

Out of nowhere, I was coughing hard—choking—and a large piece of candy slid over my windpipe. "Uh-oh," I tried to say. It was what I always tried to say when choking on candy (yes, it had happened before). But in prior instances, I had always been able to utter something.

I wasn't getting enough air, was about to black out while driving. No, not on this crap—hardly worth it. I pounded the steering wheel while attempting to say "Hello? Hello?" because I knew from my article on CPR that if you could talk, you would make it.

If person can speak, cough or breathe, do not interfere.

I grasped my throat with thumb and forefinger, the universal choking sign. Silent squeals as I struggled to clear my airways… and for the briefest moment, as I thought "Oh well, this really is it this time," a wave of calm, of death's not as bad as I thought, of fuzzy peace, washed over me… until suddenly the culprit puff dislodged.

"I can talk!" I screamed, my throat instantly sore, but laughing with tears now as I reached for a different flavor—I hadn't tried the green ones yet—then flung it, and the rest of them, over my shoulder into the back. In the rearview mirror, I looked pasty, the new, daring blush long gone, wherever it went.

I should have showered before setting off, but I hadn't wanted to return to the house. Hopefully, my parents wouldn't smell sex on me. It would be nice to spend a week with them before moving west. They had been sounding rather sprightly on the phone of late, relaxed and happy.

My folks were excited about my getting into Stanford, especially when I explained that there was a good chance I could teach a few undergraduate composition courses to subsidize my costs. Jake was busy assembling a guide for me of the Bay area, and had offered to check out housing possibilities. Soon, I would be living within an hour of the Pacific Ocean.

But my first stop was home. May would be blooming in Montclair.

> I went to the woods because I wished to live deliberately, to front only the essential facts of life, and see if I could not learn what it had to teach, and not, when I came to die, discover that I had not lived.
>
> Henry David Thoreau

I lasted only seven and a half months as a newspaper reporter, but I changed the course of Anne Arundel highway history.

Allegedly.

-30-

Acknowledgments

I could never have written this book were it not for a few quiet, intensely coffee-smelling Dunkin' Donuts franchises near my house. I also could not have written it without the interest of numerous friends and relatives who have suffered through my long career as a writer (and tennis player).

A huge debt is owed to the readers of an early draft: Nancy Gerber, Peter Hitchcock, Ina Lancman, Lise Levin, Wendy Newman, Susan Raphael, and Kathy Sherman. Their insights and constructive criticism, combined with enthusiasm, helped me see my way out of a black-ink forest. I also am grateful to the following readers of subsequent drafts for valuable feedback: Susan Crane, Helane Russo, Jane Schwartz, Carol Sherman, and Tami Sherman. Mary Jo Rhodes and Rose Sherman provided incisive, eleventh-hour suggestions, and Melanie Best provided terrific proofreading. And I would like to acknowledge several special friends for cheering me on: Mary Kay Brooks, Lisa Czolacz, Sharon Dalto, MG Denton, Tami Furman, Nancy Goodman, Susan Grant, Allyson Jankunas, and Nina Peyser.

I am very grateful to Aaron Kleinbaum for teaching me everything I know about transportation engineering; Sue Roddy for her consultation about EMT procedures; publisher Brooke Warner for her patience and guidance; and Lorna Weinstock for long-term assistance with existential angst.

Thanks to Lise Levin, Wendy Newman, Susan Raphael, and Helane Russo for more help with existential angst. To Ina Lancman and Jane Schwartz for their editorial acumen and years of bolstering conversations about books and writing. And to Nancy Gerber for providing wise counsel on three versions of my manuscript, and for letting me know on a weekly basis that she believes in me. My mom, Carol, and sister-in-law, Kathy, offered ongoing validation, and my sons, Peter and Sam Hitchcock, always provide much love and inspiration. Thanks to my brothers, Chuck and Jamey, for caring a lot about me and this book, and to my sister Tami, an amazing friend, who often understands me better than I understand myself.

I would like to extend my heartfelt appreciation to Elizabeth Kracht, my editor, whose in-depth critiques gave me more adrenalin than my beloved Dunkin' Donuts coffee and really helped me gain mastery over my material. Like an old-time editor, Liz would not let me say "I'm finished"—although I often tried!—until the work was truly done.

Most of all, I would like to thank my husband, Chris Hitchcock, who eagerly read every chapter of every version of this novel. In addition to providing love, editing, encouragement, humor, and a yearly "grant," he proved to be a terrific plot consultant as I strove to make this an even better story.

About the Author

© Steve Hockstein/HarvardStudio.com

Ellen Sherman received her MFA from the University of Iowa's Writers' Workshop, and has worked as a journalist, editor, and teacher. She also has worked as a proofreader, tutor, Girl Scout cookie counter, and training coordinator for literacy volunteers—all afternoon positions so that she could write in the mornings. Her first published novel was *Monkeys on the Bed*. Besides writing, her passions are choral singing, playing tennis, traveling, sampling new candy, and most of all, hanging out with family and friends.

The Reading Group Guide for *Just the Facts* is available at www.ellensherman.com.

SELECTED TITLES FROM SHE WRITES PRESS

She Writes Press is an independent publishing company
founded to serve women writers everywhere.
Visit us at www.shewritespress.com.

A Tight Grip: A Novel about Golf, Love Affairs, and Women of a Certain Age
by Kay Rae Chomic $16.95, 978-1-938314-76-6
As forty-six-year-old golfer Jane "Par" Parker prepares for her next tournament, she experiences a chain of events that force her to reevaluate her life.

Watchdogs by Patricia Watts
$16.95, 978-1-938314-34-6
When journalist Julia Wilkes returns to the town where her career got its start, she is forced to face some old ghosts—and some new enemies.

Clear Lake by Nan Fink Gefen
$16.95, 978-1-938314-40-7
When psychotherapist Rebecca Lev's father dies under suspicious circumstances, she becomes obsessed with discovering what happened to him.

Beautiful Garbage by Jill DiDonato
$16.95, 978-1-938314-01-8
Talented but troubled young artist Jodi Plum leaves suburbia for the excitement of the city—and is soon swept up in the sexual politics and downtown art scene of 1980s New York.

Water On the Moon by Jean P. Moore
$16.95, 978-1-938314-61-2
When her home is destroyed in a freak accident, Lidia Raven, a divorced mother of two, is plunged into a mystery that involves her entire family.

In the Shadow of Lies: An Oliver Wright Mystery Novel by M. A. Adler
$16.95, 978-1-938314-82-7
As World War II comes to a close, homicide detective Oliver Wright returns home—only to find himself caught up in the investigation of a complicated murder case rife with racial tensions.